Modern
Hebrew Literature

MODERN HEBREW LITERATURE

EDITOR IN CHIEF:
Prof. Gershon Shaked

SENIOR ENGLISH EDITOR:
Dr. Debbie Guth

LITERARY EDITOR:
Hadar Makov-Hasson

TRANSLATIONS OF REVIEWS
FROM THE HEBREW:
Philip Simpson, Mitchell
Ginsburg, Chaya Galai,
Sharonne Cohen

PUBLISHER:
The Toby Press LLC

MANAGING EDITOR:
Aloma Halter, *The* Toby Press

COVER DESIGN:
Tani Bayer, *The* Toby Press

Published by *The* Toby Press for
the Institute for the Translation
of Hebrew Literature

CORRESPONDENCE

Submissions & Editorial, please
contact:

The Institute for the Translation of
Hebrew Literature
23 Baruch Hirsch Street,
Bnei Brak, Israel

Mailing address:
POB 10051, Ramat Gan 52001, Israel

Telephone: 03-5796830
Fax: 03-5796832
litscene@ithl.org.il
www.ithl.org.il

For sales & subscriptions, please
contact *The* Toby Press

The Toby Press LLC
POB 8531, New Milford,
CT 06776-8531, USA
& POB 2455,
London WIA 5WY, England
www.tobypress.com

Modern Hebrew Literature is published
with the generous assistance of
the Culture Authority of the Israel
Ministry of Science, Culture and Sport
and with the generous assistance of the
Department for Culture and Scientific
Affairs of the Israel Ministry of Foreign
Affairs.

© 2005 The Institute for the
Translation of Hebrew Literature

Modern Hebrew Literature is indexed
in the MLA International Bibliography
of Books and Articles on Modern
Languages and Literatures and in the
Arts & Humanities Citation Index.

Typeset in Garamond by
Jerusalem Typesetting

Printed in Israel

Modern Hebrew Literature
New Series
Number 11, 2005/06
ISBN 1 59264 132 6

Acknowledgments

Reviews reprinted by courtesy of:

Maariv, for "End the Occupation" by Yaron Avitov, (28.01.05), and "Angst and Rivalry" by Ioram Melcer, (12.11.04)
Copyright © *Maariv*
Haaretz, for "All-Conquering Conflict" Ioram Melcer, (20.05.05)
Copyright © *Haaretz* Daily Newspaper Ltd.
Yedioth Ahronoth, for "The Mysterious Ivanov" by Amnon Jackont (16.07.04); "Flawed Identity" by Haya Hoffman, (11.02.05); "Daycare for the Chronically Forgetful" by Miri Paz, (26.11.04)
Copyright © Yedioth Ahronoth
Y-net, for "Wise Questions" by Ariana Melamed (*Y-net Entertainment*, 2.02.05)
Copyright © *Y-net*

Thanks to the following for permission to include excerpts and poems:

Xargol Books for an excerpt from *Tsalka's ABC* by Dan Tsalka, Copyright © Dan Tsalka and Xargol Books, 2003
Sifriat-Poalim for an excerpt from *There Comes the Light* by Lea Goldberg Copyright © *Sifriat Poalim* 1946
Maya Bejerano, Ronny Someck and Israel Pincas

Israel Pincas' "The Rain" and "The State" reprinted from *Ariel* No. 69

Special Thanks to Amos Oz
Photo of Amos Oz by Dani Machlis, by kind permission of Ben-Gurion University of the Negev

Modern Hebrew Literature is indexed in the MLA International Bibliography of Books and Articles on Modern Languages and Literatures and in the Arts & Humanities Citation Index.

Modern Hebrew Literature No. 11, Fall 2005
(RE)WRITING LOVE
in postmodern times

Contents

ix

Editorial

Love has been a dominant thread in prose and poetry since the day when shepherds sang songs of love in Song of Songs, through the time of Catullus and Petrarch, till today. Hebrew literature is no different from that of other nations; the "chosen" people do not have a unique form of love. From the first, Hebrew literature, in its modern incarnation, has tried to tie the love of the land to the love between man and woman. One of its first works was Avraham Mapu's *The Love of Zion*, which links the love of Amnon and Tamar to the longing of a man for a land he's never laid eyes on. In Bialik's generation, literary tension usually centered on love and desire, and the way the two impulses clashed with the pressures of tradition. "They say there is love in the world. What is love?" Bialik asks, describing the frustration of yeshiva boys searching for a love they would never find. Since Bialik, we have witnessed wonderful stories of love by Agnon and, later, by S. Yizhar and Moshe Shamir.

Over the course of time, our love stories have changed and grown more complex. They have distanced themselves from the topos of Zionist nationalism and the conflict between tradition and individual desire. In much of modern Hebrew literature, love is neither simple nor straightforward. We find sudden unexpected twists and turns, loves rooted in the shadows of the past, conflicts between parents and children, intimacies that question the nature of love in these postmodern times; raucous, angry loves that bear the scars of living.

This issue of *Modern Hebrew Literature* resonates with the many voices of love. The interview with Amos Oz gives us the unique perspective of the author of (most recently) *A Tale of Love and Darkness*, 2002, one of the most successful and intriguing novels published in Israel in the past few years. The poems by Maya Bejerano, Israel Pincas and Ronny Someck add varied poetic voices to our literary "conversation." Among the excerpts from novels and short stories, many of the authors are women. The generation of Zeruya Shalev, Savyon Liebrecht and Judith Katzir, among others, builds on that of Amalia Kahana-Karmon, Yehudit Hendel and Ruth Almog, and over the past few years they have brought studies of human relationships to quantitative and qualitative maturity. Many of these authors are adept at describing the complexities of human relationships. Male authors, such as Joshua Sobol, Yitzhak Ben-Ner and Alex Epstein are innovative in different ways.

It is tempting to try to categorize these authors, or at least the topics they treat, but this is often impossible. In a goodly number, love relations are shot through with conflicts from a previous life—Zeruya Shalev's protagonist longs for the marriage she gave up even as she attempts to build a new family; Edna Mazya harkens back to a lost European past, Alona Frankel recounts her life during World War II. Many deal with family relationships—Avirama Golan portrays the disintegration of two families against the background of Israeli society; Savyon Liebrecht delves into the world of a child who accompanies his father in his nightly search for a bed; Esty G. Hayim looks at suffocating motherlove; Mira Magen's protagonist lives in the shadow of his mother's abandonment, while Judith Rotem's story takes us into the world of a troubled ultra-Orthodox family. In others, romantic or sexual love stand in the fore; but in very different contexts: Judith Katzir portrays the youthful passion of a schoolgirl for her (female) teacher; Aner Shalev follows a man of mature years who has a passionate love affair with a doctoral student; Dan Tsalka ruminates on his love for art and its similarity to falling in love with a woman. In many cases, present love is inseparable from family past, while in others—such as Eshkol Nevo and Yitzhak Ben-Ner—the cohabitation of the personal with the social or political is very much in evidence.

In a more fantastic genre, Joshua Sobol plays with the various selves of Hanina, his protagonist, while Alona Kimhi's novel follows the bizarre, raunchy tales of a young dental hygienist who inherits a tiger from her Japanese lover. Finally—and as a counterpoint from another literary period—Lea Goldberg's beautiful novel, *There Comes the Light*, tells the story of a young woman falling in love with a friend of her father's who, like him, is mentally unstable. Her love is the tragic attempt to restore a father who has disappeared behind the padded doors of a mental institution.

The loves included here are thus varied, and very often troubled. The couples bear no relation to the biblical Amnon and Tamar, they are not ardent lovers of Zion or religious scholars who have lost their faith; nor are they "new Hebrews" like Elik, Moshe Shamir's famous hero, who was apparently born of the sea. They are in many cases post-Freudian and postmodern individuals who illustrate the crises of relationships in the modern Western world. In this respect, it appears that Israel is no different from other Western countries.

In all, the many faces of love reflect the cultural period. "Globalized" as well as local values are refracted in these texts. And in these postmodern times, authors—both male and female—have complex and often painful answers to Bialik's question, "What is love?"

※

ITHL deeply regrets the recent deaths of Batya Gur and Dan Tsalka. Our deepest sympathies to their families.

G.S.

Gershon Shaked is Professor Emeritus of Hebrew Literature at the Hebrew University of Jerusalem. He is the author of more than 30 books of literary criticism as well as one novel.

In Memoriam:
Ephraim Kishon

EPHRAIM KISHON, (1924–2005), one of Israel's best-loved writers abroad, was born in Hungary. He studied sculpture and painting, and later wrote for the Hungarian stage as well as publishing humorous essays. He immigrated to Israel in 1949 and started publishing in Hebrew two years later. The feature films *Sallah Shabati* and *Blaumilch Canal*, which he wrote, directed and produced, were distributed worldwide. His play, *The Marriage Contract*, had one of the longest runs ever in Israeli theater, and his sketches and plays have been performed on stage as well as on TV networks in many countries. Kishon published 42 books for adults and eight children's books. His work has been published in 37 languages and translated into 33 languages. In 1990, he was awarded the Bundesverdienstkreuz, First Class, Germany's highest award for literature, and in 2002, he received the Israel Prize for his life work. He died in January 2005.

אפרים
קישון
שעיר, לעזאזל
רומן סאטירי

The Bald Truth

Tel Aviv, Hed Arzi, 1998, 231 pp.

T his year we lost one of the great satirists of Israeli literature: Ephraim Kishon. On May 14, 1952, Kishon wrote a notice "to the masses" in *Maariv*, announcing the beginning of his new satire column, which he then wrote for years. In his writing, Kishon captured the essence of the young state, its mixture of people, the melting pot of old and new immigrants. He did not reflect on the Israeli experience using the standard approach of the time, like satirists Amos Kenan and Dan Ben Amotz, nor did he describe characters and situations recognizable only to a small elite (like the Palmach). Rather, throughout his life, Kishon addressed the situations and experiences familiar to any Tel Aviv resident who could understand "1000 words."

Kishon fought for the ordinary citizen. With his limited yet endlessly inventive vocabulary, he took on the establishment, the bureaucracy, the absurd politicization of public life, and the economic disparities in this country. He never tried to answer questions about the identity of the State after the Zionist revolution. Instead, he pushed for a European type of normalcy, and like Herzl in his day, he envisioned something along the lines of the liberal, utopian Austrian Empire.

Kishon, the new immigrant, placed our life under the microscope. He did not draw from the common storehouse of characters, the pioneering groups and fighters who defined the character of the nation in its early years. With enormous talent, he exposed the provinciality, the petty bureaucracy at the helm of the young Levantine state, and the ethnic tensions of the melting pot that never melted. His talent won him international acclaim, and his books were translated into more than thirty languages. His passing is a great loss to Israeli culture. He has, however, left behind a towering cinematic and literary legacy which will guide us into the future. May his memory be blessed.

Gershon Shaked

Ephraim Kishon
The Bald Truth

An excerpt from the novel

A few days later, in the presence of the President of the country, we representatives of the Harpoon Front were sworn in as deputy ministers in the new government. At the end of an impressive ceremony His Excellency the President invited us to a personal interview. The first citizen of the nation, a man of many talents and great wisdom, thanked us for our outstanding achievements in the matter of the defense of the national hair but at the same time, in view of the poverty and severe unemployment rampant in the country, drew our attention to the historic need to act with greater moderation towards the bald-headed with means: the moneyed classes.

"Your Excellency the President," Pappi was quicker than me to reply. "That goes without saying, in the light of both the urgency of the matter and the esteem in which we hold you. Our intensive research among the bald has long made it clear that bald-headed members of the property-owning class are more patriotically inclined than the impecunious—and probably also richer. Such people have no reason to fear for the future, but the bald-headed masses, Your Excellency, must now pay seven times over for their sins. The Harpoon Front has given its pledge."

On hearing this, the president informed us we had made a very good impression on him. His Excellency then rang the bell and summoned his tall, blonde secretary whilst we bowed and curtseyed our way out of his presence, overwhelmed by the effect of the meeting with this fascinating personality.

Our new office was named the "Government Institute for the Study of the Problem of the Bald," and had fifty rooms. These were placed at our disposal by the Ministry of the Interior, together with sixty-eight employees whose virtue, hair-wise, had been thoroughly vetted by a special government committee. On the day we assumed office, we were privileged to receive a visit from the Prime Minister, Everard Titus Dugowitz, accompanied by his stepfather, Dr Zanmaier. We had a personal discussion about current political issues:

"Take note, my friends," said the Prime Minister, "that we have absolutely no intention of deviating from the long-standing humanitarian tradition of the nation. Our country takes pride in the fact that since time immemorial we have been a law-abiding nation that works tirelessly to preserve the parliamentary rights of all its citizens. What counts with us, my dear friends, is the democratic expression of the will of the people."

"And my will too," interposed Dr Zanmaier. "Both."

"No question," said the Prime Minister. "It is in this spirit, therefore, that we must examine the possibility of preparing a bill to drastically reduce the social and economic loopholes exploited by the bald-headed fossils. This bill should be put together by your party and should not be too lenient."

"Delighted, Your Excellency." I replied at once. "It will be an honor."

We then got to work on the details of the proposed bill. We were joined in this discussion by the Minister of the Interior, Baron Dorfenhausner. Without wasting time, he made it clear that the first clause of the bill had to deal with the expiration of any foreclosure imposed by a bald man on the property of a man with hair. If a man with flowing locks, for instance, owned a villa in the fashionable area of Rose Hill and a bald-headed bank manager plotted to foreclose the mortgage on the villa because of some piddling debt of forty thousand forint, then according to the proposed law, the validity of the foreclosure would expire immediately. In effect, such a foreclosure would never be discussed before any recognized tribunal unless this was explicitly asked for by the creditor.

In the meantime we had to cope with another burning issue: apparently there was a lack of precise information about the situation of the bald in the country. We therefore approved the proposal of Dr Zanmaier and officially instructed the National Bureau of Statistics to drop everything else and devote themselves exclusively to the preparation of a detailed report on the extent of the resources of the bald-headed, giving the number of individuals bald and balding to various degrees.

In view of the fact that only a professional was capable of determining with any precision the rate of progress of baldness on the head of the average citizen, the Ministry of the Interior took our advice and set up permanent bureaus of hair science, manned by hair officers with knowledge and experience. These institutions were designed to remedy the lack of authentic information. The officers placed in charge of the bureaus were given a crash course by the government, provided they were at least twenty-two years old, with no previous convictions. And of course were crowned with a full and curly head of hair. At the same time, Pappi and I were hesitant about taking upon ourselves the formulation of the draft bill and asked Dr Zanmaier for authority to approach the Prime Minister and request the services of six eminent jurists from the University Faculty of Law.

"Everard give plenty plenty professor," was the response of Dr Zanmaier, who on the spot told his stepson to act in accordance with our instructions before the whole state system of law was endangered.

The following day the Front entered the magnificent chamber of the parliament. We took our places in the seats marked for us on the extreme right and almost every member of the legislative assembly rose to applaud this small but ideologically indomitable faction. The waves of sympathy that flowed towards us were most affecting and the oldest member of parliament, none other than the widow Schick, fell weeping on the neck of her neighbor, and stood erect only when she discovered that Pappi was standing on the other side and she had been tearfully embracing the twin brother of his masseuse.

There were of course a few members of parliament who treated us with marked hostility. We ignored them completely. At the most one of our members made a few rude, not to say obscene, gestures in their direction.

Dr Schwantz, who had been elected Deputy Speaker of the House, opened the first session. The first to present himself was Ernest Szomkoti, in a maiden speech for the party.

Pappi gave a brief description of the program of the party for the defense of the national hair, expressing the hope that the movement which so far had provided two deputy ministers would soon make available a large number of active leaders for the good of our beloved country.

"The struggle against the plague of baldness, like the ten plagues of Egypt, is a fight to the bitter end!" Pappi concluded his brilliant speech, and added: "We may be a small party, but we are also a great party, and with all my heart I pray that we may be blessed by our Father in Heaven."

After Pappi, the Prime Minister rose to make his speech. To the accompaniment of the sound of bells relayed by loudspeakers to the chamber, the leader announced that the problem of baldness would be solved by constitutional means, thanks to the firm policy of the new government, acting in close cooperation with the opposition, which had inscribed on its banner the credo of the defense of hair. An early date would therefore be set aside for a discussion of a proposed government law to deal with all aspects of the curse of baldness and cast the yoke from the necks of a working society of men with hair.

There was the enthusiastic, festive atmosphere of a real holiday in the chamber of deputies. Party leaders and active members who had only just made each other's acquaintance embraced warmly with uninhibited freedom. Some members of parliament leapt onto the benches and showered us with congratulations and new ideas and even the names of bald-headed rivals who deserved to be dealt with.

After these events the first session of parliament dissolved with the members in high spirits. The program of the Harpoon Front seemed to them the only ray of hope for the salvation of the country. The new government, sheltering in the shade of St Antal, had not succeeded in putting together any alternative programs of reform. But just as the deputies were nearing the exit from the chamber the Prime Minister, Mr E.T. Dugowitz, called on them to wait a moment, he wished to bring a message of immediate importance to their attention. That very morning, he announced, the country had embarked upon a glorious war, and fighting was already taking place near the borders of the state. Our joining the war, said the Prime Minister, guaranteed victories for the side of the great nation represented in our country by Dr Zanmaier.

"We are a fighting nation, with a famous military tradition, and this is a natural step to take," declared the Prime Minister and expressed the hope that the House would retroactively endorse the decision. At all events, an ultimatum had already been sent to half the nations of the world, for safety's sake.

At first the idea of war was greeted with a certain reservation by the citizens but within a short while they came to like the idea, to the point of seeing it as a successful device for capturing territory and expanding the borders of the country by force of arms. At any event, the sight of soldiers returning home from the conquered territory, their arms loaded with valuable gifts for the family, was a most inspiring vision.

Translated from the Hebrew by Eddie Levenston

Fiction:

Excerpts from Recently Published Novels

AVIRAMA GOLAN was born in Givatayim, Israel, in 1950. She studied literature at Tel Aviv University, specializing in translation, and later studied French language and literature while living in Paris. She worked for many years as a correspondent and editor for the daily newspaper *Davar*, then moved in 1991 to *Haaretz* where she is now senior correspondent on social and cultural affairs as well as a member of the editorial board. Since 1999, she also presents a weekly literary magazine on Channel Two TV. Avirama Golan has published four children's books, one non-fiction book, and a novel. She has also translated many children's classics and written screenplays for children's TV. Her novel, *The Ravens*, became an instant bestseller in Israel and has been awarded the Book Publishers' Association's Golden Book Prize (2005). It will be published in German and Italian. Golan is currently writing her second novel.

The Ravens

Tel Aviv, Hakibbutz Hameuchad /
Siman Kriah, 2004. 183 pp.

Avirama Golan

The Ravens

S*An excerpt from the novel*

ari asked Didi if she'd met Shimon at the university. No, said Didi, I met him long before. Where? It's a long story, ask my mother. Whenever anyone asks her, she volunteers her refined version.

Shimon was two years ahead of Didi in the regional kibbutz high school, but he wasn't one of us, he was a boarder from outside the kibbutz, and Sarka, Didi's mother, who before embarking on her nation-wide activities in the movement was regarded as an outstanding educator, called him in two or three times for a talk, because he was a boy from a difficult background. I'm not saying, God forbid, that he himself is depressive, said Sarka, but there's clearly a strong influence on the part of a self-sacrificing mother figure. Women from the Sephardi community were educated to passive suffering, she explained to the embarrassed homeroom teacher.

I think you're exaggerating, said the homeroom teacher. His father was a prominent personality in the Yishuv,[1] and Hannah—she pronounced the name with the stress on the last syllable—is not a

1. Jewish community in mandatory Palestine

17

primitive woman from an immigrant transit camp. After all, when she was young she was a member of the underground in Iraq. Who knows what she went through.

Don't get me wrong, said Sarka to the homeroom teacher. I have nothing but admiration for the boy's inner strength, and by the way, I have no doubt that he has been influenced to some extent by our basic egalitarian values, but you can't treat my instincts with contempt either.

I didn't say anything that could be interpreted as contempt, said the homeroom teacher.

Sarka is a broad-boned woman, but not fat because she is very strict with her diet. Her breasts are heavy, her face is round and her hair is drawn back and swept up in a French pleat. She is not the kind of mother who preaches. Nor is she in the habit of interfering, just as she never took pity on her daughter when she cried in the baby-house. The night nurse would come to call her, and she would tell her, let her cry a little longer, I know there are mothers who want you to call them. I'm not one of them. A little crying never hurt a baby.

She may have gone a little too far with this approach, and today opinions on the subject are divided. In any event, the daughter grew tough, but not necessarily for this reason, perhaps it was simply because she inherited Sarka's characteristics. Not those of David, who is moved to tears by every little thing, and whose lips immediately start to tremble. Anyway, that's how things turned out, and Dina, or Didi as she was called on the kibbutz—personally Sarka can't stand this name, or pet names in general—Dina grew stubborn and strong. So much so that sometimes she would shut down for days on end and refuse to cooperate with her teachers. The child doesn't accept authority easily, Sarka explained to them, at her age there's nothing wrong with it. The only problem with Dina, Sarka thinks to this day, is that she gets easily confused between reality and imagination.

I still don't understand how you met, said Sari. Didi didn't tell her. For six years, during the entire period of her studies at the kibbutz high school, she searched ceaselessly for a moment's peace and quiet, a moment to be by herself. Even the toilets were hard to get into. People stayed inside as long as they could. To gain fifteen minutes on their own. And there was always someone in the room. When she couldn't stand the suffocation, she would run away in the middle of a class. What is it now, Didi? I don't feel well. I can't breathe. Nitza the homeroom teacher would look at her suspiciously, but she didn't say anything. Didi would crawl through the hole in the fence and emerge into the orchard of blue plums behind the school.

At the beginning of summer in the tenth grade, the dark heavy soil would be cracked with dryness and covered with a bed of leaves that had not yet started to rot. In the cool shade priests' hoods and bindweed and wild fennel would sprout. The fruit pulled the branches to the ground. The plums that had ripened prematurely and not been picked, fell and split apart slowly and silently. The juicy pulp stuck to Didi's fingers. Fat bulbuls and tiny humming birds nested in the tangled growth of the honeysuckle. One minute they approached her with wary hops and flew away, the next they pecked busily. Didi lay among the trees and read *The Squaw's Revenge* and *Little Fadette*. She already knew them by heart. She should have outgrown them long ago. But nobody was going to tell her what to do. If Sarka and Nitza and Miki the house-mother had only known. But none of them knew.

Only Shimon, the silent boy from outside, found her out. He was thin, and his skin was darker than that of the kibbutz children, even though they hung out at the pool till dusk while he sat for hours on the tractor and never took off his clothes. He always wore a faded blue shirt. He sat down beside her and she trembled, and he leafed through her book and gave it back to her, and a week went by and then another, and on the third week he suddenly dared to touch her, and they still hadn't spoken a word to each other.

Her mouth and throat were dry and she was afraid. A spell led her hand to his lean body, and a spell allowed him to touch her groin until he almost hurt her, but also sent a strange vibration though her. He's the wicked robber and I'm the princess, and in the end I'll die here like this, because who knows where he comes from, and where he gets his knowledge of how to cause this forbidden pleasure.

At night, in bed, she told herself that he was forcing her. That she had no choice, and that was why she agreed. But every morning, in the middle of school, her body rose from the chair and took her to the hole in the fence.

Even before the harvesting was over, Nitza saw her once bending down next to the fence and sent her back to class with a reprimand. What does she think, that lily of the valley, that princess, she said to the school principal, that if she's Sarka's daughter she can do whatever she likes? She's not the first to step out of line with me. We've seen sluts like her before. From that day till the end of the term she wasn't allowed to leave in the middle of class, and she, in revenge, held her tongue and refused to eat. One day they served a bowl full of blue plums in the school dining hall. Blue? said Varda the fatty. What's blue here? On the inside they're completely yellow, only the skin's purple. The fact that you invented the name blue plums doesn't obligate the group. Didi swept them all onto her plate and didn't touch anything else.

You're such an egoist, said Varda. Can't you consider other people? And she went to fetch another bowl. In the evening Didi had an upset stomach and kept on throwing up, and when her fever rose they took her to the ER in Valley Hospital. When she returned she went to sleep in Sarka and David's room. On the kibbutz the rumor circulated that she had been hospitalized in the gynecological ward, you know why.

I'm not going back to school, she said. David pleaded: Dideleh, you can't set yourself apart from the group like this, but Sarka said to him, leave the child alone, a few days apart won't hurt her. I'll speak to Nitza. So what, every time she isolates herself and withdraws from the group, you'll back her up against her teachers? We're talking about normal adolescent crises here, said Sarka. There's nobody on this kibbutz with a better understanding of education than me, and with all due respect to Nitza, nobody understands the girl's psychology as well as I do.

But you don't understand anything, Mother, Didi said silently. And in the middle of the vacation, when severe menstrual pains cramped the lower half of her body, she got out of bed, put on her bathing suit, took a towel from Sarka's closet, and announced that she was going to the pool. At the end of the vacation Shimon was drafted into the army and he didn't return to the kibbutz even when he had leave. Didi didn't see him again. So what, she said to herself on the first day of eleventh grade. In the first place, nobody knows what happened there, and in the second place—what happened anyway?

Before long Didi succeeded in reversing the reputation she'd acquired as a girl who didn't fit in. By the end of school she was in a good position, thanks to sport: the long jump, the one hundred meter sprint. She always came first, or at least second. Once she came home from the championship at Sha'ar Ha-amakim with a big gold medal. David, his chin trembling, took down the beaten copper plate which had been on the wall ever since they moved into the nice house reserved for long-time members, and with slow movements, as if performing some solemn rite, hung the medal in its place. By the end of the week it was no longer there. Sarka gave it to the school and hung a bunch of mummified flowers in its place.

There's no contradiction between my struggle against blatant individualism and my support for her individual ego, she said to David. We're talking about competitiveness here, and you know very well that I consider competitive individualism out of place in an egalitarian society. The child is already seventeen, she's strong enough, it's time she understood that with us, competitive sports too are a contribution to the collective. No, no, there's no need to put the copper plate back. I could never stand it anyway.

Didi shrugged her shoulders and walked out of the room. A few months later, in the army, when she passed a sports instructors course with distinction, she forgot to invite Sarka and David to the graduation ceremony. How can you forget something like that, Dideleh, said David sadly. How should I know? she said, I was terribly tired. For god's sake, don't make a fuss. Everything was screwed up because of Yom Kippur and the war. Half the instructors are at the Suez Canal anyway. So I forgot. So what.

Sarka was silent. But a week later Didi received a reproachful letter from her: Dina, my dear. There are certain fundamental values we live by, and lying is no trivial matter. We both know very well how often I was obliged to cover up for you in front of the whole kibbutz. Perhaps I was wrong. In any case, it doesn't exempt you from responsibility. I want you to know that your father is very hurt.

The day after Didi was discharged from the army, she notified the kibbutz secretary that she wanted to leave. For a trial period. She would definitely be coming back, but she wanted to try living in the city for a bit. David arranged a job for her at a small printing press in south Tel Aviv, which belonged to a friend of his and Sarka's from their early pioneering days, and a room with a relative who lived on the second floor in Frishman Street. Didi never mentioned her name. If anyone asked she said that she was living with some woman, a widow but not so old.

Two months after coming to town, at the end of winter 1975, she went into Café Vered on Dizengoff Street for a cup of hot cocoa. Every evening she looked for a different place to pass the time until it was late, so she wouldn't have to sit with the widow. She climbed the café's curving staircase slowly and sat on the second floor. The glass lamps shed a murky yellow light, and the old people sitting round the little round tables, drinking boiling tea from glasses in decorative metal holders, looked to her greedy, spiteful and scheming. The coats hanging on the backs of their chairs gave off a smell of naphthalene, like the smell that came from the wall closet painted in beige oil-paint in the widow's apartment. She didn't know anyone, and nobody knew her.

The old feeling started settling in her stomach again. A yawning, churning whirlpool, climbing to her gullet. The kibbutz, with the mud sticking to rubber boots, with the sooty kerosene stove in the room curtained in brown and yellow stripes, lay in wait in the distance, holding out long arms and imploring her to crawl back to it. She couldn't drink the cocoa. Nausea filled her throat. She felt stifled. Now, according to the familiar sequence, she knew the pounding in her temples would begin. Afterwards the breathlessness.

Suddenly a tall thin young man climbed up the steps, and it took her a few minutes to remember who he was. He looked at her in surprise, and she smiled with an effort because of the pain tightening round her forehead and the back of her neck. He said, hi, you're

Didi from Shibolim, right? You haven't changed, and he sat down next to her, called the waitress and ordered tea and a doughnut. All this time he didn't take off his coat. He had come to meet someone, and the person hadn't showed up.

How are you? What are you doing in town?

I live not far from here.

What do you say. So you left?

Yes. But it's more or less temporary.

Why?

Because I'm not quite sure what I'm going to do. It's good that I can always go back.

He was silent. She thought he said something. What?

Yes, he said. That's how it is with you people.

And you?

I had no reason to go back there after the army.

So what are you doing?

I'm in the middle of a degree in economics, and a few months ago I started working in my father's factory. Floor tiles. No, he smiled at the face she pulled, it's actually interesting. I like it. Why are you laughing.

What do you like?

The production, taking nothing and making something from it. Don't laugh. But I'm only at the beginning.

Are you cold? he asked and touched her hand. No. Because you're shivering. It's nothing, she said and shivered harder. Afterwards he accompanied her to her room. Didi told him that she felt really strange in the city. There was nowhere to be alone. There were strangers around all the time and it bothered her. Nevertheless she didn't move from his side all evening, and the evening after that too, in the café and the cinema and even in the street, when they walked. He didn't talk much, only asked her questions, and she answered, and almost from the first evening they held hands and clung to each other. One evening they came out of a movie and it was raining and they got wet. You know, she said, it's like a picture I once saw, I don't remember exactly, but there were two people in it who were saved from a shipwreck.

23

What nonsense, he said.

Yes, she hurried to take it back. You're right, it's silly. There isn't even a sea here, we're in the middle of a park.

Translated from the Hebrew by Dalya Bilu

ZERUYA SHALEV was born in Kibbutz Kinneret. She has an MA in Biblical studies and works as a literary editor at Keshet Publishing House. Shalev has published four novels, a book of poetry and a children's book. Her bestselling novels, *Love Life* and *Husband and Wife*, have received critical acclaim both in Israel and abroad. They have been translated into 21 languages and have been bestsellers in several countries.

Shalev has been awarded the Book Publishers' Association's Gold and Platinum Prizes, the ACUM Prize for *Love Life* (1997), the German Corine Book Award (2001) and the French Amphi Award. *Husband and Wife* was nominated for the French Fémina Prize (2002) and has been included in the French Fnac list of the 200 Best Books of the Decade. *Late Family* will be published in French, German, Italian, Polish and Dutch.

Late Family (Terra)

Tel Aviv, Keshet, 2005. 403 pp.

Zeruya Shalev

Late Family

An excerpt from the novel

At the end of an avenue of bony carob trees, their limbs distorted with age and their unwanted fruits surrounding them like a disintegrating shadow, he parks his car, not far from my home, not far from the home he has left. I know the street, but not the narrow lane splitting off from it like a broken branch from a tree trunk, I have never walked down this steep slope, never stepped on the gray patches of asphalt which give rise to a feeling of neglect, as if this lane is nothing but the back yard of a superior street and not fit for habitation, only for hurrying down with the steep slope quickening your steps like a wind at your back.

The beginning of a smile at the corners of his lips as he flings open the door to the stairwell of the old concrete building, then the door to the apartment, on which his name does not yet appear, leading into a white and almost hollow space where the overpowering smell of fresh paint makes it hard to breathe. I haven't had a chance to buy furniture yet, he says, I was only here the day before yesterday and I took it at once, it's the first apartment I saw, do you like it? His voice echoes between the spotless walls, lending his voice a celebratory tone, a little forced, as if he's delivering a speech for my benefit, and I walk through the rooms, their number multiplies, it seems as if each room gives birth to another room. It's enormous, I say with wary admiration, what do you need so many rooms for, and he says, better too many than too few, no? And I say, yes, if it's possible, and nevertheless I wonder what kind of life he is imagining, after all he's at the clinic every day, and presumably the children will only be here once or twice a week, is he trying to hint at something, to signal that he has already taken us into account, me and Gili, am I now walking round the apartment destined to be my home, like a person unwittingly treading the paths of his future?

Whose room will this be? I point to a completely empty space, square and spacious, with a little porch stuck to it like a pulled out drawer left open, and he says, Maya's already chosen it, and Yotam the one next to it, and I'm happy to say they managed not to fight over the rooms, and again the insult like grains of sand in the corners of my eyes, they were here before me, his children, actually why not, it's supposed to be their home after all, and yet who is the extra room meant for, on the other side of the bedroom, where a double bed is already standing and a wide wardrobe with a mirror, in which I glanced in surprise, not used to seeing myself next to him surrounded by white air. The room isn't big, but there's a big mystery surrounding it, and when he inspects it at my side, he seems to be studying my face, expecting a question, but I quickly put an end to the half-guided tour, fall onto the sofa standing by itself in the living room, examine the view from the windows: pine trees too tall for their slender trunks, bare-boned Persian lilacs, in the spring their branches will be covered with tender green shoots, they will be transformed, like a house filling with the gleeful shouts of children, and it seems that there is nothing I want more than to be here with him in the spring, to see the trees change their mood as if by command.

Congratulations, I say, and he nods absent-mindedly, sits down next to me on the sofa, he too seems uncomfortable confronting the emptiness which has not yet made up its mind what to fill itself with, is he too thinking about the home he left, about the armchairs and sofas and carpets and paintings and bowl of red pears and notes on the refrigerator and children's voices and the murmur of muffled weeping rising from one of the rooms. It's still a little sudden for me, he says apologetically, I did it all in a hurry, before I had second thoughts, this month at the clinic was too long, I had to get back a sense of home in exchange for the home I had. And a wife in exchange for a wife? I suggest, and he repeats after me, drawing the words out as he does, a wife in exchange for a wife, perhaps, does that bother you? And I reply, not really, as long as it's me, and he says, yes, it's you, I believe it's you, but his eyes stray restlessly over the empty walls, as if he has just noticed that his creditors have confiscated all his belongings in the night, and I whisper, then why don't you make love to me? And he turns to me as if rousing himself from a daydream, but I do make love to you, I make love to you all the time, can't you feel it? And he slowly unbuttons his thin orange sweater, smiling at his exposed chest as if happy to meet an old friend.

The daylight suits you, he whispers, you look softer in the daytime, and it seems that the jeans slide off me of their own accord, willed by the flattered body eager to expose itself, like the bodies of infants restricted by their garments, and even he parts from his clothes with surprising ease, and when he gets up to pee I follow him with my eyes, the way he stands sunk in thought in front of the lavatory, and it seems as if I am watching him like then, from the doorstep of his house on that Saturday morning, with our children playing in the next room, and he is a complete stranger to me. And he comes up to me pale and ardent, draws my face to his and licks my lips, this is what should have happened that morning and look, it's happening now, even if the summer has turned into winter, and not a single leaf is left on the deciduous trees. A rare grace has fallen to our lot, to be given a second chance, to turn forbidden into permitted, and a high white wave of gratitude lifts me in his arms and flings me into the depths of this weekend, as if it is a place and not a time, the name of a distant island, the Weekend Island, which unlike the Children's Island where the children were left without their parents, is one where the parents are left without their children, for a limited time, true, to remember that selfish, pampered existence; and even Gili's words—I hate Yotam's father—lose their power, because this rare man whose hair falls gracefully onto his forehead and whose eyes are damp isn't anybody's father on this weekend, he belongs to my body abandoning itself to his movements, to my ears falling in love with his voice, to my lips clinging to his lips, to my fingers speaking to his fingers. He belongs to my body which denies the knowledge that he ever held inside him another, absolutely new human being, my vagina has forgotten that a baby ever passed through it with huge, terrible effort, my nipples stiffening to his tongue have forgotten that they were ever sucked by toothless gums, and that sweetish milk dripped from them. It is only pleasure these organs seek to produce, vapors of hot, seething pleasure, vibrations of ancient cravings howling inside them, the pealing of breast bells and the whisper of sighing skin and the moan of delight.

It isn't too soon for you, you're sure enough of me already, he whispers, and I fit myself around him like a ring, consecrating the two of us to each other with rhythmic movements, driving to the point as secret as a precious dream that vanishes on waking, yes, I'm sure of you, if only because you asked, and when the pleasure arrives, knocking on the door like a welcome guest carrying brimming baskets in his hands, it will be slow and heavy, golden as a honeycomb melting in the sun, and we'll be soft and sticky as if we're made of hot dough, steaming human dolls fresh from the oven, we'll roll over locked in an embrace, my hair in his mouth his hands on my shoulders my face in the hollow of his neck, sinking into a slumber which is neither sleep nor waking but the body's basking in the lingering memory of its happiness; and in the remembering the pleasure is doubled and tripled until it seems that the body can no longer contain it, and the apartment can no longer contain it, nor the steep narrow lane nor the street nor the entire city, groaning under the weight of the pleasure. And now the Sabbath siren wails in the windows, and although it is produced by an electronic machine it seems to issue from the heavens themselves, to take part in the marriage, to add its blessing to the blessing of the wet stones, the bare branches, and I know that every Friday evening when I hear the Sabbath siren I will remember this moment, and this moment will remember me, and even if it never returns again the knowledge that it once happened will accompany me like a prayer whose words have been forgotten, and I lean on my elbows and look at his face, and it seems that a subtle note evident only to us has been added to it, as if we have suddenly discovered a secret blood bond, a secret childhood experience, his face becomes familiar, as if he was hiding next to me there, digging a tunnel in the ground of the orange grove, a tunnel that would hide us both.

A chilly winter gloom covers the stones of the houses, the heavy darkening treetops, it seems that the rails of the radiators set in the wall are trying in vain to heat the big empty apartment, in which there is no substantial life yet, and when I reach out for the sweater lying at the foot of the sofa he grips my arm, wait, don't get dressed yet; he gets up and brings a blanket from the bedroom, a light, airy blanket, but the air sewn into it seems blazing hot, and he tucks it round my body with little pats, as if he is covering my body with sea sand, silently stroking my hair and spreading it over the cushion, yet nothing has been said, and it seems that both of us are afraid, even the words are afraid of making a mistake, of marring the magic of the evening covering the windows with darkening purple drapes as it descends.

Silently I listen to his bare footsteps as he opens the tap and fills the kettle with water, takes a cake from its packet, a knife from the drawer, a plate from the cabinet, and every movement appears more miraculous than its predecessor; and I, it seems that my limbs have forgotten how to move, lying next to me paralyzed by surprise: a voluntary lameness has come upon me, as if I have moved enough, and now that I have more interest in doing so, all I want to do is lie here on the sofa, in the regal pose in which he sculpted me, and see how good everything can be. How tasty the cake will be, how aromatic the coffee, how lovely this man who is taking care of me so naturally, how deep the satisfaction of doing nothing, new laws seem to have descended on the world, and there is no more need to make an effort, the gifts arrive one after the other, in an endless parade full of delight, and when he puts the tray down on the sofa next to me he says, now what, you can't complain any more that we haven't made love yet, and I laugh, it seems to me that I'll never complain about anything again, I'll have to find a new content for my life, and he grins, why, did you complain so much? And I say, endlessly.

About what, for instance? he asks, handing me the hot coffee. I gulp it quickly, a few drops escape from the cup, trickle down my chin and fall onto my chest. He bends down and collects them on his tongue, and I sigh, what difference does it make, what's the point of trying to remember my former life, which seems to me now like a dark narrow path, full of potholes and pits, a path whose sole purpose was to bring me to this moment, to this apartment, to this man, and with typical rashness I wipe out all the years I've lived with a wave of my hand, as if there wasn't a single worthwhile moment in them, as if no thread will stretch from my former life to my new life, no connection, no similarity; and with the arrogance of someone saved from a disaster who imagines that his happiness is now guaranteed, I repeat, what difference does it make, from now on I'll never complain about anything again, and he looks at me in amusement: promises made in bed aren't very reliable, you know, his hands play with my hair, like a child stroking a cat's fur again and again, in anticipation of the soothing purr.

Translated from the Hebrew by Dalya Bilu

ESHKOL NEVO was born in Jerusalem in 1971. He spent his child-hood in Israel and Detroit, USA. Nevo studied copywriting at the Tirza Granot School and psychology at Tel Aviv University. He worked as a copywriter for eight years and then started writing short stories. Today, he teaches creative writing and thinking at a number of academic institutions, among them the Bezalel Academy of Art and Design, Tel Aviv University, Sapir College and the Open University.

Nevo has published a collection of stories, a work of non-fiction and a bestselling novel, *Homesick*, for which he was awarded the Book Publishers' Association's Golden Book Prize in 2005. The novel will be published in French, Italian and German.

Homesick

Tel Aviv, Zmora Bitan, 2004. 361 pp.

Eshkol Nevo

Homesick

An excerpt from the novel

All of a sudden I heard a boom, says an eyewitness wearing a cardigan and breathing heavily. All of a sudden I heard a boom, says a salesman from the shoe store, an involuntary smile twitching on his cheek. A boom? What boom? An explosion doesn't go boom, just like a dog doesn't go bow-wow. At the café they say Noa never got here, and the shift manager tries to allay my blatant fear. The police blocked off the street, so even if she wants to, there's no way she can get through. Women and children among the casualties, the announcer says, his face all puffed up. And the thought flashes through my mind, what about Noa? Is she considered a woman? The ticker moves across the bottom of the screen. Downtown telephone lines crash from overload. But more than an hour's gone by. She's had enough time to get out of there and call. The telephone shrieks. Is it her? No, her mother. More uptight than I am. Yes, I heard. No, she hasn't called me. No, she doesn't take the number eighteen bus. She takes the one-fifty-four. She's probably stuck there and can't call because the lines are down. At Bezalel? There's no one there to talk to. The office is only open on odd-numbered days, and only for an hour or so. Yes, it's outrageous, I know. No, Tel Aviv's no better. You're right,

35

Yehudith, those should be our biggest problems. Right, the first one to get the all-clear signal will let the other one know, okay? Okay. I put down the receiver and start pacing, unable to turn off the TV and unable to watch it because I'm afraid there'll suddenly be a close-up of a gurney with Noa on it. The man in the picture hanging on the living room wall is still staring at nothing at all. Maybe he's waiting for a phone call too. Noa's right. That picture is a depressing sight. If she gets out of this okay, I'm taking it down. Why did I say "if"? I look in the refrigerator for something to eat. The sticker "Create or Stagnate" screams at me from the corkboard. I find two rubbery dried apricots. I sink my teeth into one of them, toss the other into the air. And catch it. Sima's baby Lilach is sobbing, screaming. Her crying splits walls. In my little workroom, the book *Psychopathology* is open to the chapter on post-traumatic stress syndrome. I browse through it till I get to the chapter on behavioral therapy for worry. I don't read, just put it down belly up, open to the right chapter. The phone screams. Now it has to be Noa, and I am going to give her a piece of my mind. Why didn't she call sooner? It's Hila. Noa was supposed to have called her in the morning from the café to set up a day of Reiki, but no sign of life from her yet. And the café isn't far from Jaffa Street, you know. Yes, Hila, I know. Are you watching TV? Yes. The mayor's giving a speech to a sea cucumber. "The horrendous sights…" "On a day like this…" "We did everything we could…" People are crowded around him like fans around a soccer player. It's terrible, Amir, Hila whispers into my ear, just terrible. How much hate does a person have to have to do such a thing? It spreads so much bad karma in the world. Didn't they ever hear of non-violent protests? If they would just march, lock arms and march, no one could stop them. I don't know, Hila, I don't know if things like that work in the Middle East, I say, and hear myself sounding as hollow as a political analyst on TV. She'll be okay, won't she? Hila begs. Let me know if you hear anything from her, Amir. Promise? Yes, I promise. Bye Hila. Bye. The Minister of Something-or-Other Affairs promises, on live TV, to bring the full weight of justice to bear on the terrorists and those who send them. The fans are pushing. The camera is shaking. The broadcast switches back to the studio. They rehash everything we already know. What if she doesn't call? Scenarios start to blossom in my mind and I can't trim them down. Noa with an amputated leg, Noa with crutches, Noa in a hospital bed with me beside her reading her the end of *A Hundred Years of Solitude*, trying to absorb fact that I have a handicapped girlfriend. And another one: Noa's dead, someone informs me, a police officer. He calls and offers me his condolences. (Is that how it works? They offer their condolences even before you know you need them?) Then he asks me to come to the hospital. My trip to Shaare Tzedek Hospital—no, to Hadassah Hospital in Ein Kerem—is ceremonious. Cars make way for me as if they know. Her family is already waiting at Hadassah Ein Kerem—it's not clear how they got here before me. A quick hug with her father. A three-way hug with her mother and sister. They're all weepy and I can't shed a tear. Why not? And why does that whole scenario infuse me with a kind of sweetness, why does it excite me? A knocking at the door saves me from the answer. Three quick, demanding knocks. I open it. Sima apologizes for bothering me. I just wanted to ask if Noa's all right, she says, brushing her hair from side to side with one hand. In the other, she's rocking Lilach. Why are you standing outside? Come in, I extend an arm and she comes in. Dressed nicely, sharply creased black pants, a pink blouse with buttons down the front, one of them open right over her cleavage. Is that what she wears at home? I take a quick look at the living room through her eyes. The two pillows on the couch. No underpants on the floor. It's a good thing I managed to straighten up a little in the morning. Did you hear anything from her? she asks, putting Lilach down on the rug. The fear starts creeping again. No, I haven't heard anything. Tell me, that café of hers, isn't it near…? Yes. And…? She never got there, I checked. *Allah yestur*, God help us, Sima says and puts her hand on her breast, her fingers slipping under her blouse through the open button. Meanwhile, Lilach discovers my tennis ball. She feels it with her fingers and tries to eat the yellow fuzz. Sima bends down (plain white bra) and takes it out of her hand. It doesn't taste good, she tells her gently, it doesn't taste good. She hands me the spit-soaked ball and says, with the same gentleness, don't worry, it'll be okay, it's not her bus. Sit down, why are you standing, I say to her and ask myself till what age will my heart respond so quickly to maternal gentleness? I wonder if even when I'm eighty, I'll want to rest my head between the breasts of every woman who talks to me that way. Did you call the emergency numbers yet? Sima asks and points to the screen. I look for a pen that writes and manage to copy down only one number before the broadcast switches to 'our correspondent, Gil Littman' with the first pictures from Shaare Tzedek Hospital. Gil Littman taught us field studies in high school, and all the girls in the class used to put on lipstick before his lesson. Now he's talking to the hospital's Deputy Director, with infusions and white gurneys racing past in the background. They'll probably postpone Avram's operation again, Sima mumbles to herself. Who'll have time for his kidneys now? You never know, I try to reassure her, staring at the screen and thinking: Just don't let any black hair pop up now. No black hair. I start imagining again: I'm at Noa's bed stroking her hair, kissing the veins on the back of her hand, and she doesn't wake up. Doesn't wake up.

Thirty-four injured, Sima says, repeating the number the Deputy Director has just said as if it were a mantra for self-relaxation. Thirty-four.

As I dial the first number on the page, I recall those stories from Memorial Day programs about mothers who feel in their bodies, even before the army officers knock on their doors, that their son has been killed. Did Yotam's mother feel it too?

I check to see what I'm feeling inside my body, and find turmoil.

Translated from the Hebrew by Sondra Silverston

JOSHUA SOBOL was born in Tel Mond, Israel, in 1939. As a young man, he was active in the socialist Hashomer Hatzair youth movement. After being a member of a kibbutz from 1957–1965, he went to Paris and studied philosophy at the Sorbonne. A leading Hebrew playwright, Sobol has been artistic director of the Haifa Municipal Theater; he has also taught esthetics and directed theater workshops at Tel Aviv University as well as at various colleges. He has written 13 plays, many of which have been staged in Europe and the USA to great critical acclaim. *Soul of a Jew* was performed at the Edinburgh, Berlin and Chicago Festivals. *Ghetto* was named Britain's "Play of the Year" in 1989, and has been staged in Vienna, Cologne, Toronto, Oslo, Paris, Los Angeles, Berlin and Washington. Most recently, his play, *Witness* was performed at the Heidelberg Theater Festival, 2005. Sobol has also published two novels, *Silence* (2000) and *Whiskey's Fine* (2004). His work has been translated into nine languages.

יהושע סובול
ויסקי זה בסדר

Whiskey's Fine

Tel Aviv, Hakibbutz Hameuchad /
Siman Kriah, 2004. 239 pp.

Joshua Sobol

Whiskey's Fine

An excerpt from the novel

Nobody loved Hanina. Hanina was once in love with a woman, but even when he loved he wasn't beloved. There was nothing about him that people love to love. Hanina himself, a sturdily built man, didn't love any of the two hundred and forty- eight body parts he had received from nature, and he refused to accept his body until he had laboriously reshaped every single part of it. Be it his jaws or his chin, his fingers or his toes. Already as a youngster his legs seemed to him too short and thick. Exhausting exercise, cruel self-discipline, endurance developed to the limits of the ability of the nervous system to bear pain—and even beyond, to the point where the pain is so intense that it numbs pain—finally resulted in the ability of his short legs to carry him distances that Olympic long-distance runners could only dream of, and his terrifying kicks sent more than a few believers, who had joyfully joined the holy war in the knowledge that the pleasures of this world are very small compared to those of the next, as promised in the Repentance Sura of the Koran, to Paradise.

The shortness of his legs had stopped bothering him long ago, and their remarkable power, of which we will hear more later, had turned into a source of private amusement and practical jokes, such as the limp he simply adopted, and which he now abandoned as he entered the elegant store. He made for the men's department and proceeded to the suits section with a springy, almost dancing, step, his darting eyes boldly appraising the shapely sales assistants and challenging them: let's see you recognize me now, Winnie. If you've got any sense, we'll have a secret that Mister Adonis, who sent me to you, doesn't know. Who are you, Winnie? Are you the slender black sales assistant with the ample breasts and the shaved head? Or are you the other one, the one with the childish face and the boyish haircut, wasp-waisted and stringy limbed, like the long-legged Segestria Perfida spider?

While his eyes are darting from one to the other, the black sales assistant approaches him and asks how she can help him.

I'm looking for a black cashmere suit, he says in a French accent.

She asks for his size and as he answers her the long-legged spidery wasp intervenes and points out to her colleague that this dangerous man belongs to the impudent race of the short-legged. She conveys this strange diagnosis in a whisper, but she makes sure that it will reach his ears. The provocation is like a surprising opening move in a game of chess.

Wait until you see how thick they are, he winks at the treacherous spider with his non-aiming left eye, while his aiming eye, which has seen the whites of the eyes of quite a few men in the last second of their lives, penetrates her with the sharpness of a laser beam.

I can't wait to see! The long-legged spider laughs suggestively, and adds a question:

Hey, who are you spending the holiday with?

With a nameless secret friend, says Shakespeare.

Wow, the spider exclaims enthusiastically, a nameless secret friend! I'm dying to meet him!

He's standing in front of you on two short legs, which are just long enough to reach from his ass to the floor.

I'm spending the holiday alone with a nameless secret friend too, says the Segestria spider.

The question is whether we'll be alone together or apart, says Shakespeare.

Being alone on Christmas is like being a parrot in a cage in a deserted pub, whistling "Strangers in the Night" to itself, says the spider with the stringy limbs.

They exchange cell phone numbers, and after abandoning the idea of the suit, he sets out for his meeting with the director of public relations in the pharmaceutical firm.

Hanina emerges into the city, where a wintry wind is raging, actually howling in the narrow passages quarried through it by the skyscrapers like tunnels in the bowels of a mountain. He strides down the street illuminated by thousands of sparkling Christmas lights, and as he calls the young sales assistant on his cell phone the fingers of his left hand play with the packet of Sol Leyeles's pills in his pocket.

Hi honey, he says, this is the dangerous man with the short leg here.

Hi, she says, do you want to come round?

If you want me to.

Very much, she says, but I have to warn you that it will cost you something.

Sure, he says, in this life the only thing you get for nothing is death.

It's five hundred dollars till midnight, or a thousand for the whole night.

Including breakfast? he asks.

You're a real piece of work! She laughs with a sound of tinkling bells from the other side of the satellite wandering through space. For you—including breakfast.

Dinner is on me, he says after she gives him the address. And he adds: Including red wine.

❧

After clicking three locks and drawing back two bolts, she opens the door and sways and shies away from him like a praying mantis in brief black running pants and a black tank top, all arms and legs of a still growing adolescent girl. Her long skinny legs grow like two bamboo canes from black Doc Martens, high and heavy, as if she has just returned from a hike in the country. The contrast between the clumsy masculine boots and the stork legs underlines her boyish appearance, and he wonders if he isn't getting involved with a minor here. The wide bracelets on her wrists draw his attention to the vein-slashing scars underneath them. He looks up and meets her narrowed eyes, weepy eyes that examine him with feline curiosity. She sees that he has registered the scars and sends him a smile that may be naive or embarrassed, or maybe it comes from bottomless sadness and terrible bitterness, because her full lips stay sealed when she smiles, and he asks himself if they express sensuality or disgust, and the narrowed weepy eyes, are they alive or dead? A dark grasshopper silhouette against a background of Manhattan's sea of lights, whose waves break against the glass of the huge picture window, which takes up the entire facade of the one-room apartment, whose area he estimates with a comprehensive glance at thirty-five square meters. He notes to himself that there is only one entrance, that the kitchenette adjoins the living space with no dividing wall, takes a quick look inside the open bathroom door to make sure there's nobody there—and thus, in the habit acquired during the years of pursuit and liquidation, he concludes the screening procedure and answers the questionnaire he internalized during those stormy years, the strict compliance with whose details saved his life and the lives of the members of his team, until the Alsatian caught it in India, and Jonas ended his life in the team's last liquidation operation, in the terrible pursuit in the desert of Tino the Syrian, who he is now trying to reach through this young woman, facing him here in all the enigma of her youth. He hands her the bottle of Côtes-de-Ventoux he bought in the wine shop on the corner of 14th street, and says:

Half's yours, the rest's mine.

And when she laughs, and starts tearing off the paper, and he is sure that this apartment is not a trap—only then he closes the front door behind him and takes care to bolt at least one of the locks.

You don't have to worry about the window, says the perfidious spider, who picks up on his warning and control system with the senses of an alley cat, you're on the twenty-first floor, and that window doesn't open.

That's fortunate, he says without going into details, but her sad smile confirms that she has taken in everything unsaid hiding behind the single word, and they both know that both of their suicidal pasts are now filling the empty space between them.

In the meantime she strips the bottle of its wrapping, and the tissue paper rustles in the silence.

Coat de Ventooks! she cries in a New York accent.

You know it?

I'm not sure, she hesitates, although the name rings a bell.

Have you ever been to Combs d'Arnevel? he asks.

Comb Darnavel? No, where is it?

In France, he says, in the North-East of the province of Châteauneuf du Pape, this wine comes from there, and I almost died there.

What from?

An agricultural problem, he says. Somebody wanted to fertilize a vineyard with my corpse. I preferred him to fertilize it with his.

And we're going to drink his blood tonight? she says provocatively.

Are you a vegetarian?

Do I look like a vegetarian? she says with a wry smile.

No, he admits. Although it would be all right even if you were.

From what point of view?

This wine goes well with lamb, fish and vegetarian dishes as well.

You took all eventualities into account, she expresses her appreciation.

It's become my second nature, he reassures her.

Since that night in the vineyards of Arnevel? she guesses.

Long before that, he says.

But since then you celebrate with this wine?

When I take a risk.

Do you feel threatened?

Yes, he admits. Very threatened.

By me? she asks.

No, he says. By my id.

Do you still believe in Freud? she asks.

Who do you believe in? he asks her in return.

Who do you expect me to believe in after my Lacanian therapist tried to persuade me that it was okay to try to commit suicide, if that was the first step I had to take in the process of my individuation in order to be who I am? She laughs with weepy eyes.

A Lacanian therapist in New York?!

He's Hispanic, she explains. He was a student in Paris in the sixties, a student of Guattari and as crazy as him. Anti-psychiatrist, anti-philosopher, anti-human.

What's his name?

What does it matter, she says dismissively, Ramon Gasparo, a name to forget. He would tell you that you're simply afraid to fall in love, because the thing you call your id, is the sexual attraction and the sex that begins in the place where the ego ends.

This spider is a trap, he says to himself. She's a lot more sophisticated than she looks, or else she's just trying to make an impression with a bit of bullshit she learnt by heart to turn on clients looking for an intellectual whore.

So, she says, was that just an overture, or is your id really threatening your ego?

The whole system, he says, trying to access the depth and breadth of this consciousness confronting him. Dangerous volcanic activity has been taking place lately, deep down in the bowels of the mountain, far below the tunnels and shafts of the abandoned mine.

Take a hot bath with lavender oil, she suggests, and relax.

I'll leave the door open, he says.

It doesn't bother me, she reassures him.

She starts filling the bath.

Translated from the Hebrew by Dalya Bilu

ANER SHALEV was born in Kibbutz Kinneret in 1958. He studied mathematics and philosophy at the Hebrew University of Jerusalem and received a Ph.D in pure mathematics in 1988. In 1992, after a postdoctoral fellowship at Oxford, he joined the Einstein Institute of Mathematics at the Hebrew University where he is now full professor, and served as chairman of the Institute from 1999 to 2001. Shalev has lectured at universities around the world, including Princeton, Yale, Oxford, Paris, Chicago, London, Cambridge, Chicago and Berkeley. He was a guest speaker at the International Congress of Mathematicians in Berlin in 1998, and has also lectured at a number of literary conferences. Shalev has published two books of short stories and a novel, *Dark Matter*, which will be published in German and Italian. In 1985, he was awarded the Harry Hershon Prize for his first book of stories.

Dark Matter

Tel Aviv, Zmora Bitan, 2004. 284 pp.

Aner Shalev

Dark Matter

W *An excerpt from the novel*

hen he reflected on that week in New York, which lasted seven days in spite of his tendency to see it as an eternity, the dramatic moments would flash before his eyes, or the symbolic moments, but never the simple, everyday moments, even though they were presumably the main thing, like running past the seductive shelves of the supermarket in Bleecker Street, with her sitting in the shopping cart, shrieking like a child, or crossing Washington Square at six in the evening with the shopping bags in their hands and a rosy apple in her mouth, or searching for the ideal frozen yogurt, with just the right degree of density, and the dedication with which she drank it, with a spoon, without losing a single drop, or going up to the hotel room in the miniature elevator, and her always lively dialogues with the doorman when handing over the key, no, moments like these hardly ever occurred to him, perhaps because there was nothing dramatic about them, or symbolic, yes, what mainly preoccupied him were the symbols, for instance the snow which suddenly fell, when they were going up to the top of the Twin Towers building, for just five minutes, and stopped the minute they came down, or the accident with the bottle of champagne they planned on drinking together in the bathtub, and everything that happened in its wake.

To this day it isn't clear to him who was to blame for the incident, he was the one who made the bottle fall off the bureau, but she was the one who opened the bottle without telling him, and put it down so close to the edge of the bureau that in hindsight you could say that it was a joint project, spilling the champagne, like so many of the other incidents, despite the temptation to find a single guilty party, and when he reflected on these incidents, these dramatic or symbolic moments, and on the procession of coincidences that left them no choice, and the cumulative effect of these moments, and the causal connections between them, for example the ants that arrived in the wake of the champagne which had soaked into the carpet, and grew into an army which marched all the way to their bed and invaded the very bedclothes in which they were sleeping, he would immediately realize that it wasn't the events themselves that disturbed him, but their symbolism, their ostensible meaning, because with ants and a champagne-soaked carpet he could cope, but not with the cumulative weight of the symbols, symbols which he himself insisted on implanting into events that were presumably completely neutral in themselves, like for instance the fact that during all that week in New York it didn't snow once, except for those five minutes when they were standing on the roof of the Twin Towers building.

He had taken an extended Thanksgiving break from work, and told Ruth that he was flying to Washington for a series of meetings, which in fact he often did, only this time, instead of flying to Washington, he stayed in New York and booked a small room in a hotel next to Washington Square. He was surprised that Ruth accepted his trip to Washington unquestioningly, without turning a hair, it was the last Thursday in November after all, Thanksgiving, a strange time for business meetings, and when they were having coffee in their big kitchen an hour before he left the house he rehearsed possible answers to her possible questions, but she only asked if the coffee was sweet enough, and afterwards she helped him pack, and when she put two business suits into his green suitcase he nearly said, what for, I won't wear them anyway, and then it occurred to him that this was the price for lying, the need to burden himself with two heavy business suits, and he zipped up the suitcase in a hurry, as if to hide its contents, and when he kissed Ruth at the front door she pressed herself to his body for a moment, and he felt her black curls on his neck, and suddenly he thought that perhaps he wouldn't go, he could still unpack the suitcase and stay at home, he could still spend Thanksgiving with her, but she had already pressed the elevator button.

You know I prefer the stairs, he said to her, but the suitcase is heavy, she replied, and he picked up the suitcase and said, no, actually it isn't heavy, and suddenly he felt the weight of the two superfluous business suits and said, you know what, maybe you're right, perhaps the elevator would be better, as if this concession, and his willingness to take the elevator, scored him points in a kind of wordless game that they had been playing now for years, and Ruth said, I'll come down with you, and they sank from the tenth floor to the gilded lobby in the gilded elevator, and smiled at the doorman sitting behind a little desk at the front entrance to the building with a funny peaked cap that made him look like a policeman, and the doorman said, have a nice trip, and Adam tensed, how did the doorman know about his trip? He hadn't said anything to him, but then he realized that the suitcase in his hand and the orange Carmel cab waiting outside the building didn't leave a lot of options, and he thanked the doorman and asked him if he would be staying there for Thanksgiving, and the doorman said, that's life, sir, the job comes first, and he nearly blurted out, never mind, I'm not going anywhere either, but the cab driver who was already waiting in the lobby snatched the suitcase from him almost violently, and within seconds they were already sailing down the street, but before they set off Ruth handed him an apple for the journey and a coupon for a three dollar reduction from the Carmel Cab Company, which he had presumably received on his previous trip.

JFK? asked the taxi driver, and Adam tensed again, too many people knew about his plans, but then he remembered that it was Ruth who had ordered the cab, and she had apparently been required

to give the destination, that was the standard procedure, and he hesi-
tated for a moment, trying to gain time, studying the newsstand on
the corner, pretending that he hadn't heard the question, and at the
same time feeling a certain resentment at this unreasonable demand
for people to state their destination in advance, what do we know
about our destination, after all.

They drove west along 57th Street, crossed First Avenue in
silence, and he said to himself that up to now everything had gone
smoothly, the driver hadn't repeated his question, but then it occurred
to him that the question had been rhetorical, the driver had already
received his instructions and he was going to JFK in any case, and
if he, Adam, didn't tell him to change direction at once, in two
minutes he would find himself crossing Queensboro Bridge, and he
broke the long silence into which they had settled and said to the
driver, excuse me, I think I've forgotten something, and the driver
said, don't worry, I'll take you home, and Adam cried in alarm, no,
no, not home, to the office, there's something I have to get at the
office, and the driver said, okay, there's no need to yell, just give me
the address and I'll take you there.

He could have asked the driver to take him to Washington
Square, where the hotel was, he could have told him that that was
where he worked, the driver didn't know him after all, and there were
plenty of people who worked next to Washington Square, at NYU for
example, he could easily be one of the professors who worked at NYU,
but something prevented him from lying and he gave the driver the
address of the consulate, and the driver said, no problem, I'll get
you there, and all the way to the consulate Adam tried to persuade
himself that the consulate was instead of JFK, that the driver had
already given up on JFK, but the minute they arrived at the corner
of 42nd Street and Second Avenue and stopped in front of the ugly
blackened building of the Israeli Consulate it transpired that there
was nothing he could do about it, nothing would deter this taxi driver
from taking him to JFK, whether directly or indirectly, like some kind
of missile homing in on its target.

I'll wait here, the driver said, go get what you need and then we'll go on to JFK, and Adam said, it could take a while, maybe I should get off here, and the driver said, don't worry, I won't charge you extra, take your time, I'll wait, and Adam tried a final escape route and said to the driver, you can go, I'll pay you for the trip to JFK, I'll pay you as if you took me to JFK, and suddenly the word JFK sounded to him like some kind of mantra which had cast a spell on both him and the driver, and from now on they would go on repeating it as if bewitched, but it seemed that the last suggestion had done more harm than good, because the driver snapped in an offended tone, Mister, I don't do things like that.

When he got out of the cab, leaving his suitcase in the trunk, he reflected how surprising and unexpected life was, instead of the hotel room he had reserved for Eva and himself in Washington Square, here he was on the corner of 42nd Street and Second Avenue, the stretch opposite the consulate that had changed its name to Yitzhak Rabin Way, and on the Thursday of Thanksgiving weekend, he hoped that the place would be completely deserted and readied himself for all the security rituals of entering the consulate building, the buzzers, the double doors, the magnetic card, when all of a sudden the Consul General himself came out of the entrance and walked towards him, short and balding but full of energy as usual, and the consul slapped him heartily on the shoulder and asked him, Adam, what brings you here on the twenty-fifth of November, haven't you heard that it's Thanksgiving today? And Adam said, just some material I forgot to take home, and the consul said, material? What material? I hope you remember the procedures, and Adam smiled and pushed the magnetic card into the groove, but the door didn't open, and he asked himself if the consul had cancelled his security clearance on the spur of the moment.

He smiled at the consul, and the consul smiled at him and said, you put it in backwards, can't you see it's in backwards? And Adam turned the magnetic card around and inserted it in the groove again, and suddenly it annoyed him that he was the suspect here, he could just as well have suspected the consul, or explained to him how to insert the magnetic card in the groove, but it appeared that the consul had other ideas in his head, Adam, he said, I have a fantastic Château Musar that you have to taste, the 1982 vintage, I got a case at a special price, perhaps you'd like a bottle for your Thanksgiving dinner this evening? I'm sure Ruth will love it, it's a real bargain, and Adam said, thank you, but Ruth's going to Long Island to be with her brother on Thanksgiving, and the consul asked, what, she's going alone? And Adam said, no, I meant to say that we're both going, we took a week's leave, a breather from all the pressures of New York, and the consul slapped his shoulder and said, tell me, Adam, how do you do it? You've already been married for over ten years and you still look as if you're on your honeymoon.

Perhaps the secret is taking vacations together, said Adam, and the consul sighed and said, you're right, I travel too much, and always alone, my wife always prefers to stay in New York, sometimes it seems as if she's married to New York, not to me, and he held out the bottle again, take it, take it with you to Ruth's brother, it's a great gift, from the vineyards of Lebanon, and it'll go well with the turkey, and Adam said, the truth is that Ruth's brother isn't allowed to drink red wine, he has some medical problem, and the consul said, I have white wine as well, but it won't go with the turkey, and Adam said, right! unable to contain his relief, and the consul said, forget about Thanksgiving, next week, when you get back from your vacation, drop into my office and we'll taste the Château Musar together.

When he walked down the deserted corridor to his office on the thirteenth floor it occurred to him to check his email now, he usually checked it at least once a day, but he hadn't done it yet today, so this was his chance, because who knows, perhaps there was some important message waiting for him, maybe a new email Eva had sent him on the day of her flight, and why not check, he had time, especially since he had warned the driver that he wouldn't be back right away, but when he reached his room and sat down in front of the computer he peeked out of the window and saw the orange Carmel cab waiting for him as if he was a prisoner on leave, and suddenly he was sorry he hadn't taken the suitcase with him, if the suitcase had been with him he could have removed the two business suits and left them in the office, and then slipped out of the consulate through the emergency exit taking the suitcase with him, and freed himself from this cab at long last, and spared himself JFK, but on second thought he realized that the driver wouldn't have allowed him to the take the suitcase in any event, that his suitcase was lying there in the trunk as a hostage.

Did you find what you needed? the driver asked him on his return, and Adam said, yes, now we can go to JFK, and the driver said, don't worry, it won't cost you anything, this detour, and he cursed himself for having fallen into the hands of such a pure, moral character, any normal cab driver would have taken his money and saved him the trip to JFK long ago, only this guy was some kind of Pope in disguise, and they drove dozens of blocks south, and then got onto the Williamsburg Bridge, and he looked at the gray East river below him, and at Manhattan looming up behind him like a forest of clumsy antennae, and thought that he really should have taken advantage of the unexpected visit to his office to check his email, it was a mistake to have wasted those precious minutes on washing his face and sitting unproductively on the toilet.

They were already not far from the terminal, and the driver asked him, it's American Airlines, right? And once more it became clear that this driver knew things about him that he didn't even know himself, he hadn't made any flight reservations, nor did he recollect mentioning any specific airline to Ruth, he could no longer remember what he had actually said to her and what he had only intended saying in case she asked, or perhaps she had remembered from previous occasions that he flew to Washington with American Airlines, where he had frequent flyer points, and he avoided giving the driver an unequivocal reply and said, okay, you can let me off at American Airlines, as if everything was open and this was only one of many possibilities, and when he got out of the cab he gave him a big tip and hurried away, but the driver shouted after him and pointed at the trunk, and Adam went back and the driver gave him his suitcase and said, have a pleasant flight, and he said, thank you, and thought it's a good thing that this driver doesn't know how to fly, otherwise he would insist on flying him all the way to Washington.

Where are you flying to sir? A pretty flight attendant asked him even before he entered the terminal, and he realized that there was simply no end to this chain of errors, and that if he didn't do something drastic on the spot in order to stop this snowball it would go on rolling until it landed him in Washington...

Translated from the Hebrew by Dalya Bilu

MIRA MAGEN was born in Kfar Saba, Israel, to a religious family. She studied psychology and sociology before turning to nursing. She worked as a nurse at Hadassah Hospital in Jerusalem. Magen started writing in the early 1990s. She has published a collection of short stories and four bestselling novels. Her books have been translated into German. Magen was awarded the Prime Minister's Prize in 2005.

פרפרים בגשם
מירה מגן

The Glass Butterfly

Jerusalem, Keter, 2005. 294 pp.

Mira Magen

The Glass Butterfly

An excerpt from the novel

She opened the door to him and he was pleased to find her barefoot, without makeup, wearing broad white trousers and a faded T-shirt. The closer she came to her natural self, the younger she looked than her twenty-nine years.

"What's happening to you, you look seventy," she laughed.

What's happening to him? Life. The way it's happening to all of them. He went to the mirror and discovered she was right; he was dishevelled, unshaven, his eyes bloodshot with no spark in them. She came up behind him and asked what she was supposed to look for in an old codger like him, and he felt her breasts against his back and smelt the orange in her mouth.

"I ask myself the same question." He bent down, and hoisted her on his back. She yelled, "What do you think you're doing, I'm falling," and clutched the nape of his neck. With his burden on his shoulders he ran round the dining-table, as her bare feet flailed in the air, "What's got into you, I'm going to fall…" He held her thighs tightly against him and laughed his thick laugh, ran with her to the corridor and back again, rounded the dining table and collided with it, knocking over a pile of books that stood on it, then turned towards her bedroom, depositing both of them on the bed. Over her shoulder, on her bedside cabinet, he saw her doctor's name-tag, the watch, the bracelets, the stethoscope, the pens, the ruler. Her best clothes were hung haphazardly on the back of the chair and her high-heeled shoes lay on the floor, one face down and the other on its side. She came home and discarded everything that defines her status, he thought, and now she's just a woman and she's with me and she's wearing baggy pants and a T-shirt, and not even those now. She lifted the T-shirt over her head, and pulled her trousers down by hooking her toes in the leg bottoms, and she was naked and she said to him "Come."

Be happy, you fool, you have everything you could have hoped for, he thought, and drew her to him. Her skin smooth and cool, her breasts heavy, her legs strong, her stomach… Be happy, you fool, the events of your day have disappeared and you're already forgetting where you came from and where you're going, all this healthy and vibrant abundance of yours, and you're swallowing and being swallowed, and knowing that the words "love" and "mine" which escape from you between breaths are notes that you're going to have difficulty cashing in. A diagonal light filtered in from the dining area and lit up one pert breast, the other was in darkness. He laid his thigh on her stomach and wrapped his leg around her, feeling her pulse in his flank as he had felt it before in his back, when he carried her. Be happy, you fool, this is the best thing that has happened to you today.

You should know. These may well be the same words as those said to him [as a child] by the bare footed man with the long neck when he felt his mother Eva's little bust pulsating against his back. He called her Lady Adam and larked around with her on the roof, where he sat beside them on the concrete and ate bamba. "Stand here," the man said to her and put her against the wall, turned his back on her, spread his legs and stooped, gripped her thighs, lifted her up and ran with her around the roof, while she pressed hard against his back, wrapped her thin arms around his neck and laughed. Her curls and her dress flew up to the sky and the man pointed his chin heavenwards and shouted: "Be jealous God, be jealous!" She laughed. "I think you must have fallen on your head, really. You're absolutely crazy…"

He saw their giddy antics and was scared. The man's feet hardly touched the concrete, her hair brushed the clouds and any moment now they would take off from the roof, soar away like birds, rise so high they would be poppy seeds in the sky, tiny black dots fading. Their feet were poised for the launch, when suddenly she noticed the frightened child, the torn bag at his feet and the bamba berries scattered on the concrete.

"What's the matter with you, he's only giving me a piggy-back." She slid off the man's back and came to him full of enthusiasm, wiping away his tears with the back of her hand. "Did you think he was doing me some harm? Come on, get on my back, you'll see how much fun it is." She bent down to his height and he shrugged his shoulders, his legs like solid, immovable blocks. "Well, what's up with you, get up and we'll give you a spin." She turned her skinny back to him, held out her arms behind, grabbed him and lifted him onto her back. He shouted "No" and squirmed in an effort to free himself but she had already straightened up and was running with him around the broad space of the roof. In a panic he yelled "Don't want this," not daring to release the grip of his little hands on her neck and push away her hair which was blowing across his face, sticking to his tears and mixing with his saliva. She hoisted him up from her back to her shoulders, put his legs in front of her and he kicked her small bust and clung tightly to her warm nape, finding himself higher now than the balustrade. The street that was revealed before his eyes dried up his tears and stifled the cries in his mouth. Tiny people were running around down there, the unruly tops of casuarinas were festooned with the cords of a deflated balloon and a torn kite, the metallic hoods of the street-lamps gleamed, a dog the size of an ant barked, and garbage cans were like cola-cans. His hands moved from her neck and clutched both her cheeks, he rested his little chin on the top of her head and looked at what was above and what below, and she ran with him across the concrete. "You see, you see how nice a piggy-back can be?" The man with the long neck smoked a cigarette and watched her. "You're an animal, an animal from the jungle," he said, and turned away to look at the street below.

"Well, you've seen how nice it is, so why are you wailing at me?" she panted, clutching him by the ankles, and he squeezed his thighs against her bony shoulders, took one hand away and stretched it up to touch the sky. She slowed, but his little shoes drummed against her chest and spurred her to carry on. "More piggy-back," he pleaded, and the man with the long neck stubbed out his cigarette on the balustrade and said, "Well, Lady Adam," and she retorted abruptly, "Well what, what's the matter with you?" and quickened her pace and ran from one end of the roof to the other and stopped there, lifted the child up from her shoulders and put him down on the roof where he stood unsteadily, detached the lock of her hair that had stuck to his tongue, bent down to pick up the empty bag of bamba and the bag lying on the bare concrete, and straightened up ready to go.

"Come on, Lady Adam, we'll be late, leave him with your mother and let's go," said the man, and she said, "Yes, sure," entrusted him into the care of Mama Ruth and went.

"Mama Ruth, give me a piggy-back," he pleaded, and Mama Ruth couldn't bend down to his level, so she told him to stand on a chair. "Well, get on then," she said, stretching out her broad back for him, and he put his hands on her shoulders and hung on, moving himself up until he had his thighs wrapped round her neck with his feet out in front of her, resting on her big soft bust. She went down with him to the yard, bearing her burden carefully, "Hold on to me tight, Shamandarik, you hear me?" He put the palms of his hands on her sweaty brow and his head brushed against the lower cones of the pine. Mama Ruth walked slowly, reminding him of a camel that he'd seen in an illustrated film, with the rider kicking the flanks of the camel to urge him on and the camel breaking into a run. "Hey, why are you kicking me there?" she protested, grabbing his little sandals to stop them pummelling her breasts. "What is this, do you think I'm a giraffe?"

"No, you're a camel."

She laughed and her back shook. "I'm falling, Mama Ruth,"

he dug his heels into her chest, and her laugh climbed from her ribs to her shoulders and puffed up her neck.

"You're not falling, you're just being cheeky, and stop hitting me with your sandals there, it hurts. A camel, eh, no more and no less, a camel," and she laughed some more.

"A camel," he grinned aloud, immersed as he was in Eliana's perfumed hair.

"What camel?" she shook herself, propping herself up on one elbow and then letting it go and lying back on the sheet. Some day the feet of a child will beat at her glorious bust, he thought, but it won't be any child of mine. He kissed her on the forehead. She's going to give her child an elegant piggy-back, upright, proud, confident. Eva's piggy-back was an express train, and Mama Ruth's was a freight train, while Eliana's will be the Rolls Royce of piggy-backs. And who said it won't be his child? Take this moment and leave what is still in the future, he told himself, but the feet of the child who would one day be born to Eliana were pounding in his brain. The thought of another man giving her a child was unbearable. What's stopping him saying to her here and at this very moment, come on let's get married. Her eyelashes flickered over the stubble that he hadn't shaved. He breathed her warm neck and thought, I'm alone, and she's alone too, even if she doesn't realize it. They are all alone, even the man who hitches and welds his life to the life of his loved one and has a child with her and sleeps with her in the same bed as long as he lives and lays a heavy head full of problems on her chest. Which isn't going to happen, as he will always be left with quotas of fear and despair that he can't extricate from within himself and share with her on an equal footing. He can't even share the intensity of his joy. I've never laid my head on anyone, and all of my spiritual inventories I have counted and classified by myself, even refusing a plate of potatoes from Mama Ruth, the woman who would be prepared to crack the skies and scrape the blue off them for me. Day after day sitting facing each other in her kitchen, a loaf of bread between us, eating fried potatoes in silence, finger not summoning up the courage to touch finger. Her heart goes out to me and she eats her portion and loves me quietly, from within, from somewhere deeper than the place where the potatoes she swallows go down to. She calls me Shamandarik, and maintains brief hand-contact with every acre of potatoes that we consume. "Mama Ruth, pass me the salt," I say, because loneliness is squeezing in between us, putting bony elbows on the table and prodding us. "The horseradish too," I say, because loneliness can't endure silence, it swells up and becomes dense and stifling. It's only when we rise from the table and put our plates in the sink and go about our own concerns that our lungs are opened and we breathe fresh and sparse air.

And as for me, knowing the way that I am, living as a couple will be to me like those potato suppers, melancholy and heart-wrenching, and it won't diminish my isolation, it will double it.

He put her delicate fingers in his mouth and thought, it isn't reasonable to decide for her, "I'm not having it and neither are you." Her breathing is relaxed, her neck soft and warm, it's good for me and good for her at this moment, in this room, in this bed. Good for her? Yes. He had no doubt. And yet, though it was good for both of them, he saw the future standing by the headboard and casting a brooding shadow over the bed. She apparently saw it too, because she suddenly sat up. "Come on, let's get up and go and have something to eat," she sprang from the bed and stood there naked, rummaging among the sheets for her T-shirt. What an idiot I am, he thought, sitting up and kicking a sheet away. Concentrate on what you have here and now, on the love you were making just a moment ago and you are still panting from, on the omelet that you'll soon be eating with the woman you love.

Translated from the Hebrew by Philip Simpson

ALEX EPSTEIN was born in Leningrad (now St. Petersburg), in 1971, and came to Israel in 1980. He currently lives in Tel Aviv. Epstein has published one volume of poems, four collections of short stories, three novels, one novella and a book for children. He writes for the literary supplements of *Haaretz* and *Yedioth Ahronoth*. Epstein was awarded the Prime Minister's Prize in 2003.

Blue Has No South

Tel Aviv, Am Oved, 2005. 215 pp.

Alex Epstein

Blue Has No South

Very Short Stories

Sleeping Positions

The rocket ship was sucked into outer space years ago. Its transmissions have grown infrequent. The cosmonaut sends regards to his wife and reports that, even in a state of zero gravity, in his dreams, he still wakes at her side, in a different position than when he went to sleep.

A One-Book Woman

It's always a blind date when you meet your muse. But one night in October, two weeks after her birthday, a woman pulled a new book from a stack. One of the characters told the man she loved: "All your life you've been searching for yourself in a second-hand book." For a brief, yet-clear-enough-to-be-labeled-unsettling moment, something in that exchange reminded her of her past relationship with a man who felt his life was wasting away, even though he didn't know a single dead language. She folded down the corner of one of the pages and thought: "What if she and I switched places, taking each others' roles; would he notice?" She continued to read. At times the book was a bit sugary for her taste (at long last he responded: "And each time I find you.") Towards the end of the book she came to another page—it, too, had a folded corner.

Love is a Pocket-Sized Book in a Foreign Language

The age of electronic paper is almost upon us. All that remains are small consolation ceremonies which aren't intended to bump fate, that ghost from the future, off course: to wander the streets and look for any old book lost on one of the benches, pick it up, read a bit, and, before putting it back down, to place a bookmark between its pages—a thin branch or a yellow leaf. The woman with the weathered lipstick, for whom I wrote these lines, told me she once found an old metro card from a European capital with plenty of fares left on it in a pocket-sized book on a train. We sat next to each other; we tried to reach for the courage to ask the name of the stop the other needed. With time we learnt to ignore the monotonous voice that announced to all the other riders: "Caution, closing doors. Mind the gap."

Translated from the Hebrew by Mitchell Ginsburg

The Angel that Brod and Kafka Dreamt Of

Once, Max Brod dreamt of an angel who had only one wing. The angel knocked on Brod's door and asked him where Kafka lived. Max Brod gave the angel directions and thought in his dream that the one-winged angel was the most horrifying thing he had ever seen. The next day Brod met Kafka and Kafka told him that the previous night he had dreamt of an angel with no wings, who had asked for Max Brod's address.

The Flawed Symmetry of Romeo and Juliet

The symmetry between Romeo and Juliet (the only lovers who see each other dead) is marred only when Juliet, breathing her last breath with the dagger already embedded in her breast, looks into the open eyes of dead Romeo. Earlier, Romeo had looked at her, certain that she, like a goddess who never was (and certainly never walked among us, her shoulders slightly bent with commonplace, everyday worries: the grayish smoke of buses, the few stars that have gone missing, and yes, the great, great muddling of things which the dead poets, without blinking an eye, call love) died with her eyes closed.

The Crippled Angel

The crippled angel sat in a wheelchair especially designed for such winged creatures and chain-smoked. From his regular spot in the plaza before the museum, he watched with concern those going inside. He was trying to guess who was intending to hang himself in one of the exhibition halls.

Translated from the Hebrew by Rachel Tzvia Back

ALONA KIMHI was born in Lvov, Ukraine, in 1966 and came to Israel with her family in 1972. Following her graduation from the Beit Zvi Academy for Performing Arts, she became a stage and film actress. In 1993, Kimhi started writing plays, lyrics and articles. Since 1996, she has published a collection of short stories, two novels and a book for children. Her books have been translated into 12 languages. Kimhi's first collection of stories, *I, Anastasia*, was awarded the ACUM Book of the Year Prize (1996); her first novel, *Weeping Susannah* (1999), received the Bernstein Prize as well as the WIZO Prize in France. In 2001, Kimhi was awarded the Prime Minister's Prize. *Lily La Tigresse* will be published in French, German, Italian and Portuguese.

Lily La Tigresse

Jerusalem, Keter, 2004. 284 pp.

Alona Kimhi

Lily La Tigresse

I
An excerpt from the novel

have kneaded this dense bit of the past over and over again in my memory, until all that I have left is a jazz improvisation with unraveled edges. I try to identify the basic theme.

But it's only the memory of a memory.

Twelve years back. A transatlantic flight at an altitude of x feet above ground. Eighteen years old, on my way to the realization of my parents' army enlistment gift—three and a half weeks at a state of the art health farm in upstate New York.

This was the first time we had ever embarked on such a substantial parting. Although the weight loss program was only due to last a few weeks my parents experienced this period of time, taken together with the mileage of an entire ocean dividing us from each other, as a rupture so drastic that the finishing line, although less than a month away, blurred into a menacing and misty future, as if I had been sent deep into enemy territory with Red Army troops, and nobody knew if I would ever return.

My belongings were packed in two suitcases, one vast and green, made of synthetic material, used on our few family trips; the second was borrowed from my grandmother, an ancient rectangular monster made of fake crocodile skin, whose zippers tended to come unzipped from the wrong end, and which was consequently secured by my father, lengthwise and breadthwise, with a rope purchased at our neighborhood hardware store.

Equipped with this elegant pair of items and escorted by my parents I set off in a taxi for the airport, looking forward to the moment when I could say goodbye to them and rest from the exhausting effort of keeping calm as they plied me with more and more instructions about how to conduct myself safely and maturely while abroad.

But the future quickly proved that my impatience and arrogant self-confidence were premature. Not for nothing had my mother's and father's faces turned pale with worry when they parted from me at the Ben Gurion terminal; the moment the Boeing started to take off I was shaken to the core by the first anxiety attack of my life.

"Let me off!" I yelled at the two wispy-bearded young men in ultra-Orthodox attire sitting next to me. The air refused to find its way to my lungs, my limbs trembled in the certain knowledge of approaching death, and the sweat pouring off me sent steam rising into the interior of the plane like an Icelandic geyser.

In vain the flight attendants with their blue eye-shadow tried to fan me with the duty-free brochures, to blot my brow with scented wipes, and to find a doctor among the passengers. My anxiety in the face of their efforts was as persistent as toothache. In a final counsel of despair they decided that if I was dying, I might as well do it in more luxurious circumstances, and they moved me to the business class.

Their gamble paid off—my fear soon left me as I let my body sink limply into the comfortable seat. I learnt the dizzying power of luxury to ameliorate existential distress—the hum of the giant engines quickly turned into a soft, friendly purr, and I imagined I was hearing the sound of the waves of the Mediterranean sea spread out calmly beneath us. After swallowing one of two sleeping pills given me by my mother, I fell asleep.

I woke up only at the end of the stopover in Paris, with my friends the flight attendants walking up and down the aisles and try-ing to hide their impatience as they asked the passengers again and again to fasten their safely belts. With bleary eyes I examined my new neighbor, who displayed exemplary obedience and sat absorbed in his book, belted up and ready to fly. All I knew about Japanese tourists was the fact that they smiled and took photographs a lot, and I was about to forgo a stricter and longer-lasting scrutiny, but the intrusiveness of the enforced physical intimacy prevented me from carrying out my decision. I very soon found myself inspecting his hands holding the book, which seemed too big for his body—strong, smooth-skinned, rectangular fingers, unlined even at the joints, as if he were made of rubber. Greenish veins marked a map of winding rivers on the back of the hand. Very pale, flat fingernails completed the synthetic impression, and only the faint tremor of the fingers verified their humanity. In his sitting position I could see that he was not particularly tall. He was wearing an expensive sweater which exposed a neck the shade of wax paper, it too possessing the same artificial, flawless quality. His exotic profile, almost without a depression at the bridge of the nose, its thick lips saved from feminine sensuality only by their stern expression, was absorbed in the last pages of his book, covered with a hieroglyphic script. After he finished reading and closed the book, I was astonished to discover on the jacket the weary, melancholy, dandified, cross-legged figure of Marcel Proust.

The Japanese man sensed my stare and turned to face me.

"Sometimes humanity simply disgusts me," he said after it seemed to him that he had read my silent question.

His voice had a rusty, unsteady timbre, testifying to the childish soprano it had presumably possessed in the not too distant past. His eyes were narrow and so long that their outer corners appeared to be sliding onto his temples. Pointed, curving lashes, like those of a cartoon character, softened the foreign appearance given him by the Asiatic slant of his eyes and the heavy eyelids hooding them. His hair was cropped short and stood up in a soft brush on his head. He seemed about my age, which allowed me to immediately feel a slight superiority and to take an ironic tone.

"What humanity are you referring to?"

His slanting Mickey Mouse eyes gave me a chilly look.

"Love. It's so human. You're a slave to something whose nature you don't even understand, but to which you have no choice but to submit, because you're a human being and that's how nature, or God, or the devil knows what, made you."

The flight attendant approached us with the drinks trolley, and with smiling familiarity handed me the tomato juice she had already learnt to know as "my drink." And then for the first time I saw the flat face of my neighbor lose its stiffness and quicken into an expression of thoughtful self-indulgence.

"I think I'll have the Dom Crystal, but only if it's very well chilled."

For long months afterwards this moment seemed to me the moment when the usual reality test deserted me in favor of the secret, hidden test, in which the other loses his objective qualities and is revealed to us in the full glory of his uniqueness. The pouting lips and wrinkled nose of the expression that preceded the choice of champagne betrayed a foreign, aristocratic cultivation, which I had read about in the books of my childhood and which was intended for the rearing of little lords and princes. Before my eyes I saw children in puffy velvet trousers and lace collars drooping over consumptive chests, whose lives were led according to strict rules, and who were accompanied by stern private tutors and needed at least three maids to accomplish their morning toilet. I wanted to know everything about the Japanese Lord Fauntleroy. I made haste to exchange the plebeian tomato juice for the select brand of champagne.

I learnt that he was twenty, a native of Tokyo, that he was on his way to completing his studies in philosophy and mathematics in a program leading directly to a doctorate in philosophy. His melodious name—Momotaro—was the name of the hero of a children's book, a child born from a peach pit. I was immediately granted the privilege of calling him Taro and quickly took advantage of it, melting at the foreign taste on my tongue, until I sounded so obsequious to myself that I stopped.

The fact that his father wasn't a duke but a plastic surgeon made no difference at all to my conviction that I was talking to an aristocrat born and bred.

With fateful symmetry Taro too expressed his admiration,

which in my opinion lacked all justification, when he heard that my parents were actors. At first I tried to explain to him how lacking in glamour the status of the Yiddish theater was in Israel, but I soon gave up the attempt and allowed myself to bask in my new position as the daughter of a bohemian theater family. I entertained him with stories of the humdrum routine of my parents' lives, until his slitty black eyes grew slightly round. My chosen profession is on the scientific side of the scale and my natural tendency is against exaggerating: lies, even the most essential ones, cause me too much embarrassment for me to be able to enjoy their fruits. But now, not without the help of a few long-stemmed glasses, I allowed myself a modest degree of license, turning my parents from homebodies as dull as flannel slippers into a couple of eccentric stars, always too busy with rehearsals and tours but making up for it with their theatrical charm, which they brought home with them as well. Borne along on gentle waves of intoxication I endowed my parents with all they could ever have wished for, transforming my mother into a cool, aloof star, so light and slender that even at her age she was given the roles of young women, lovers and rebels, to play, and my father into a classical leading man, not the sensual, heavy fisted kind, but the intelligent, nervous type required to play heroes whose souls are ripped apart by powerful forces and torn in two, or even three. I expanded the repertoire of the Yiddish theater to include classics of the international stage, expressed my reservations about some of the choices made by my father in the role of Macbeth, in which he had recently been cast, and described the emotionally and physically draining ordeal undergone by my mother in developing the role of Nastasia Filipovna in an original Yiddish adaptation of *The Idiot*.

If my parents had only known what magnificent careers I was making up for them, the two old hams who couldn't even get cast as extras in the production of *A Hassaneh in Shtetl*, and who only went on getting any parts at all because of their short stature, which enabled them to play boys and girls, and their fine voices, without which you didn't stand a chance in the Yiddish shows, where people were always breaking into song. In the stories I embroidered for the ears of my new Asian friend even Monya Schneiderman, the shady

manager of their regular theater group, turned into a kind of Yiddish
Peter Brook, a gifted and idealistic director fighting to keep Yiddish
culture alive in the face of the stiff-necked Israeli opposition.

Again memory sticks out a provocative tongue at me. What
came before what, and how? Did the conversation flow from the word
go, or was I shy at first in the face of that serious gaze, too serious
for a boy of twenty? What impressed me more—his exotic origins,
or the firmness with which he expressed his opinions on conceptual
art, on free choice and the use made of it, on the intuitive knowledge
of good and evil?

When did we desist from our exhausting efforts to impress
one another, and when did the conversation turn into a volley of
enthralled question marks—Nabokov? Fitzgerald? Shakespeare? *The
Godfather? The Shop Around the Corner?* Erich Kastner? *Tom and
Jerry?* The Sex Pistols? Brothers, sisters, lovers? Television yes or no?
Is money important? Should we order more champagne or have we
already gone too far by a long chalk?

And at precisely what woozy moment did I confess to him
my youthful lust for Mike Burstyn, the popular actor, singer and
heart-throb with roots in the Yiddish theater, his pictures that still
covered the walls of my room, the erotic arousal I felt when I looked
at them, identifying in the object of my desire a stimulating combination of the glamour and virtuosity behooving a true star with
manly seriousness of the kind that inspires confidence and readiness
for long term commitment.

Did I become addicted to his existence when he told me with a
frown how he had worked last summer in his plastic-surgeon father's
clinic lugging tubs full of lumps of fatty tissue and bleeding pieces of
human flesh, or did it happen when we were locked in the stainless
steel toilet, our hands tearing savagely at zippers and buttons, tongues
and teeth in cannibalistic pursuit of ear lobes and nipples, clumsy
fingers digging in the moisture of exposed nerves.

For the first time in my life I became acquainted with the
ancient wisdom that the finest, most magnificent quarry of them all
is the male body. And in harmony with this discovery, the bubbles
of carbon dioxide from the champagne filling my blood helped me

to overcome the embarrassment I have always felt at that inglorious and unshapely quarry which is my own body. In the midst of this geological commotion I helped him to penetrate me, almost disappointed by the lack of the anticipated pain, keeping my eyes open with an effort beneath his gaze. So weak, exposed, and dominated did I feel under that gaze that I tried to diminish the moment with an ironic question.

"And isn't this too human for your taste?"

But he ignored my affected disdain and commanded in a low, breathless voice, "Lean back a little, like that, I want to touch you." And from that moment I stopped defending myself.

Thanks to the skill acquired by years of practice with Grandma Rachela's showerhead I had no difficulty in locating zones, angles and spots that rescued the occasion from all those clumsy mishaps reported by my more experienced girlfriends, both past and future. In a fit of insane, drunken courage I decided to forgo moans, tossing back of the head and other expressions of pleasure which I knew well from cinema screens and which I had convincingly reconstructed in my previous experiments, lacking in penetration, with select boys from high school or soldiers from the neighborhood.

And that encounter, the Boeing 747 lavatory encounter with the unique individual called Momotaro Okazaki, was one of those rare romantic encounters in which the teeth of the key fit with perfect naturalness into the complex groove of the master lock.

Without a doubt, we both chose the same thing: concentration. Full concentration, pushing aside every superfluous gesture or movement, imbued with the deliberate effort to avoid faking, disguise or ostentation. A concentration that distorted our faces and bodies, which refused to deviate from the path marked out somewhere in the depths of our limbic brains, which dates back to the time when we were cold-blooded reptiles. With eyes alternately opening and closing we tried to ignore the shamelessness of our doubles in the mirror.

And if some scientist familiar with the most deviant possibilities of the human body should ask how, in the name of God, a fattish girl succeeded in losing her virginity in a cubicle no more than one a half square meters in size, and how come her bum didn't slide off the edge of the sink while the flat stomach of the Japanese boy moved backwards and forwards between her marshmallow thighs, I wouldn't know how to answer him. For answers demand thought, order and sequence, and all I knew then, at the height of however many feet it was above the Atlantic Ocean, were circles of pleasure and light.

Nor would I be able to say when the pain hit me. Was it when I saw his gray sweater merging into the crowds of people at Kennedy airport, or was I still playing then with thoughts of the delightful adventure that had come my way, and only when I shut the door of my room in the weight loss clinic behind me that I understood what had happened, and it was then that I burst into the weeping that bears within it the recognition that the loss is eternal. Sealed off forever.

Translated from the Hebrew by Dalya Bilu

SAVYON LIEBRECHT was born in Munich, Germany, in 1948, to Holocaust survivor parents who immigrated to Israel soon afterwards. She studied philosophy and literature at Tel Aviv University and began publishing in 1986. She writes novels, stories, television scripts and plays. In 1987, she received the Alterman Award for her first collection of stories; two of her television scripts have also received awards.

Liebrecht has published six collections of stories and novellas, and two novels. Her work has been translated into 12 languages.

The Women My Father Knew

Jerusalem, Keter, 2005. 235 pp.

Savyon Liebrecht

The Women My Father Knew

An excerpt from the novel

That night, Meir recalled those months of wandering and the many women, his father's lovers, friends and acquaintances, who had opened their doors and sometimes their hearts to offer the man a bed and the boy a refuge.

Sometimes, when his father had apparently been given a hint that he should take his son and get out of the apartment, he'd pack his sparse belongings in a small bag, check the contents of Meir's backpack, take him by the hand and lead him down office corridors in search of a new place. When none was found for them during the day, they'd go to Kassit in the early evening. They'd stop at the tree across the street from the café like tourists putting down their bags for a minute to gaze at the scenery and study the people sitting there so leisurely, heads tilted to emit streams of smoke and gales of laughter. His father would scan the place. First, he'd check the poets' table to make sure that Alterman had arrived and to see who was sitting with him. Then his gaze would move more slowly from table to table, linger on the women sitting alone, pass over the ones sitting in couples, sort the people like a magician preparing his accessories, using his hidden senses to locate the chosen woman, the one who, within an hour, would offer her house key to the handsome man she had just seen sitting with the poets, the woman whose heart would soften upon hearing the story of the little boy who carried all his earthly possessions in his school bag. At a particular moment, his father would tense up like a hunter hearing the rustle of an animal that had wandered into the range of his rifle, catching his breath as he imagined what would follow, and Meir would sometimes be infected with incomprehensible excitement. Then, without taking his eyes off the café, his father would say, "You don't move from here, Meir. Even if it takes a long time—you wait here for me and you don't take even one step." Then he'd cross the street to the café, walking with the brisk determination of someone late for an appointment, and without turning to look back at the boy standing near the tree, he would signal him with a small movement of his hand. And Meir, breathless with happiness at the secret sign, at the pact with his father and their adventure, which was as thrilling as any of Huckleberry Finn's, would prepare himself for a long wait.

His father would stop at the entrance to the café and Meir knew without being told: from there he could assess the mood of Alterman and the people sitting at his table, the danger he should expect based on how hungry they were for amusement. Sometimes Meir could sense from across the street and through the café windows how the people at the table mocked his father, not by taunting a harmful somebody but by disregarding a harmless nobody.

"Why do they always laugh when you talk to them?" he once asked his father.

"They're not really laughing; that's just the way it is among friends," was his father's evasive reply. "One time it was because of a poem I published and now it's because of "Raisin-Hill," which is what Rosinberg means. Alterman likes to call people names and they think it's funny. So every time he calls me "Aharon Raisin-Hill," I call him "Natan Old-Man," which is what Alterman means." He raised his chin as if he had retaliated with a double dose and erased the insult. But Meir could sense the hesitation in his posture when he stopped at the door to check out the mood or level of drunkenness at Alterman's table. If he thought Alterman was in a good mood, he'd walk by them and stop to say hello before he headed for the chosen woman. When he thought they seemed eager to insult, he'd ignore them and sit down at a table that was back-to-back or side-by-side with the table the chosen woman was sitting at. Once, his heart filling with joy, Meir had seen how Alterman invited his father to the table with a generous gesture of his hand and moved his chair aside to make room for him, and how his father had sat down between Alterman and a young poet from Jerusalem. His father had sung that young poet's praises for a long time afterwards. But as the time passed, his sense of pride at the warm reception was replaced by concern that his father might get so carried away by the conversation, by the liquor that Alterman was pouring with his own hands, and by the laughter around the table, that it would get very late, and they'd still have to spend the night in Berl's cellar.

Sometimes his father would be devious: he wouldn't go straight to the chosen woman or even glance at her table. From the door, he would head for other people, pat three of them on the shoulder, exchange a few words with one of them and burst out laughing; sometimes he'd sit down next to them for a while, sip from a shot glass they handed him, then call the waiter over amiably and point to a table at the other side of the café, next to the woman's table, where he wanted his coffee to be brought. Stepping lightly, he'd move like a dancer between the tables and, still not looking at her, he'd sit down, take out a small pad and a pen and begin to write. From where he stood, Meir could see the woman looking out of the corner of her eye at his father, who was immersed in his papers. When his coffee arrived and he'd thanked the waiter with a smiling nod, a page would slide off his table and land next to her foot. She'd look at it, almost leaning over it, and when his father bent quickly to pick it up, he found himself face to face with the woman. He didn't hear what they said to each other, but Meir saw the woman burst into happy, embarrassed laughter. His father would pick up the piece of paper, return to his table and immediately become engrossed in his writing again. Still smiling, the woman waited for him to look up and would then say something to him. His father looked at her seriously for a moment, as if still absorbed in his writing, but he'd quickly shake himself free of his preoccupation and conversation flowed freely between them until she motioned to the chair next to her and he gathered up his papers and his cup of coffee and moved them to her table, where she had already made room for him. Sometimes they'd talk for a long time, sometimes he'd reach out to touch her hair or her hand, and sometimes, especially when he was a bit drunk, he'd reach under the table to touch her legs. From a distance, Meir followed the process, step by step: his father's fox-like expression as he debated silently how far he could go with this woman, his hand moving slowly to her knees under the table, her initial drawing away, the way she froze, the moment comprehension dawned, her face straining to remain impassive, her eyes slowly beginning to smile, then his wrist disappearing under her skirt, her thighs shifting to the side to shake off his groping hand, and then both his hands emerging onto the table, side by side, as if parading their innocence to the entire world.

While his father was busy seducing the woman, Meir would stand in the dark, leaning against the tree, his legs digging into the ring of sand around it. The back of his neck pressed on a knob that jutted out from the tree and he rubbed against it, moving his head from side to side. Sometimes he stood that way for a long time, sometimes his eyes burned or his legs were heavy. Sometimes people walked by and he would panic when he saw a boy from his class or a man he knew, and he'd scrunch up against the tree and tuck in his head so they wouldn't recognize him. He kept his eyes on his father and, already familiar with the entire courtship dance, watched him working hard to provide them with a place for the night, for the Sabbath, for a few days, a decent place where they could shower with hot water and sleep between sheets. On rare occasions, it became clear too late that his father had gambled on the wrong woman, like the time a woman had asked for the boy to come into the café. His father had sat him down across from them and ordered him a mug of hot cocoa, and for a moment, they looked like a small family, until the woman sprang to her feet as if she wanted to go to the ladies room, but instead, walked decisively to the door and left—and the illusion of ordinariness dissolved. That night, because they got hold of some money, they were saved from Berl's cellar floor and went to sleep in a cheap hotel.

Once, after his father had drunk more whiskeys than usual, Meir saw him get up from the poets' table and sit down next a woman wearing a green coat. It seemed as if they hadn't spoken more than a sentence or two when he got up and crossed the street without looking at the cars driving by and gesticulated at Meir, who was sitting in the circle of sand around the tree. Certain of his victory, he was drunker than usual and trembling in a way that his son had learned to recognize. He kneeled in front of him and whispered to the boy sitting on the ground, "You saw where I was sitting before?"

"Yes."

"Not next to Alterman."

"I saw, the other table."

"The table on the far left with the woman in the green coat. I'm going back there—"

"Where does she live?"

"We're about to find out. Now I'm going back there and you watch her knees."

"Why?" Meir asked, startled.

"So you can see right away whether or not we have a place tonight."

"How will I know?"

"If her knees are together like they are now, then we don't have a place. But if her knees move, each in a different direction, and there's a space in the middle, then our chances are good."

"Why?"

"Because a woman who wants, moves her knees," his father said, coming closer and blowing a smelly cloud of alcohol at him.

"What does she want?" Meir asked, averting his head.

"What I can give her."

Silently, Meir looked at the woman's knees pressed together.

"Do you understand, Meir?" his father asked, resting his hand on Meir's face. His hand smelled too.

"Yes."

"So wait here and watch. I can't see you from inside, but I know you're standing here and I'll wave to you," his father said and wobbled back to the café.

After a while, his eyes tired from straining, Meir saw from where he was standing that the woman's knees began to move under the table, pressed together, shifting together to the right and together to the left, not still for a minute, until he could see clearly how they separated, leaving a space between them and remaining that way till his father came out to him and said, "You can go inside if you need to pee. We have a place on Nordau Street tonight, two houses down from where Alterman lives."

Translated from the Hebrew by Sondra Silverston

EDNA MAZYA was born in Tel Aviv, in 1949. She studied theater
and philosophy, and received her MA in theater and cinema from
Tel Aviv University, where she later taught dramatic writing. A
scriptwriter and playwright, Mazya has also published two novels.
Several of her plays have been produced abroad. Her first novel has
been published in English, German and Italian. It will also appear
shortly in French. In 1997, Mazya received the Margalit Prize for her
play *Family Story*.

עדנה מזי"א
רומן משפחתי

The Unsatisfied

Tel Aviv, Keshet,
forthcoming 2005. ca. 300 pp.

Edna Mazya

The Unsatisfied

An excerpt from the novel

THE THIRTIES, HEIDELBERG

"Come and live with me," Robert whispered to Ruth's back. She was standing at the window and staring at the thick light of a rainy October day. The words drifted limply through the air, as neutral as if he had offered her a cigarette. As he spoke his right hand reached out, in what immediately seemed to him a ridiculous gesture, like the outstretched palm of a beggar. He withdrew his hand, clenched his lips, and waited for her reaction. She said nothing, her back erect and indifferent, or so it seemed to him. His ears burned with regret, mainly because he hadn't really meant for her to come and live with him. It was the boredom that had shrouded the whole day, without sex, without drugs, and with the only miserable little girl in the other room, which had led to the need for drama. Or so he preferred to think at this moment, when defeat demanded not only a realignment of forces but mainly a plan of attack.

According to the map of relations between them, she was supposed, if not to go down on her bended knees in gratitude, at least to turn round to face him, open her eyes wide, and ask him if he really meant his sensational offer. But she went on standing at the window like a sphinx oblivious to the trivia of this world, and his regret was therefore transformed into hostility. He wondered how best to insult her, seeking a cold, indifferent insult which would atone for his beggarly proposal and restore his pride.

"You've put on weight," he said lightly at last. She spun round as if stung.

"Where?"

Her businesslike tone, in which he was unable to detect any personal note, swelled his hostility.

"In general," he said casually, "but try to see it in proportion. There are worse things in the world. Open a newspaper."

For her part Ruth didn't hear his proposal, which she had in fact been waiting for, rather apprehensively, for the past two and a half years, because she was absorbed in gloomy thoughts about her daughter sleeping in the next room. It was the remark about her weight which had roused her. The stab of the insult fitted naturally into the depressing and decadent atmosphere of the whole afternoon. Now she was paying for the idiotic idea of dragging the child here so as not to miss a moment of the torment of his love—and without alcohol or drugs into the bargain, in a bitter and flaw-finding sobriety. She should have left long ago, but as usual, the worse things got, the higher and more convoluted her hopes became of repairing the damage.

She looked for an ugly answer that would bring an ugly satisfaction but nothing came to mind. In the meantime she displayed indifference. She stifled a pretended yawn and said that she would make tea.

Tea. He interpreted this as an attempt on her part to retreat into everyday life. It hurt him more than the refusal itself. He produced a counter-yawn, big and rude, and said that he was dying to sleep, and would she make sure the door was locked when she left. In order to demonstrate his counter-return to daily life, he began to tell her the story of the resistant lock that responded only to a violent slam. As he fell onto the bed he added, that there was nothing in the world, in the world, he stressed, which he loved more than sleeping. Before staging a hasty dropping off, he took off his boots in order to avoid the impression that he was escaping into sleep.

The icy wind that blew from his direction would have frozen less nervous souls than hers. She closed her eyes and abandoned herself to the emptiness, to be suffered like the presence of an oppressive but intimate relative. At this moment the future appeared to her as a dark, futile, undifferentiated blur, but when she turned to look at him, about to fall unconcernedly asleep in her face, the emptiness filled with anger which was immediately suppressed. She commenced careful, deliberate hostilities.

"You know," she said in a tone tinged with sadness, "there's something I've been meaning to tell you all day, but I'm fond of you and it hurts me to upset your charming self-satisfaction."

"So don't tell me," he muttered indifferently, as if at this moment she had caught him at the height of his complacency.

"Okay, I won't tell you."

"What!" He opened his eyes.

"It... it's not something simple."

"Well, what is it?"

She was pleased. He was awake and in suspense.

"It isn't easy for me to tell you this." Now she adopted a pitying, sanctimonious tone.

His long, eroded body rose before his brain had time to order it to relax. In the course of the uncontrolled movement he overturned the brimming ashtray. He cursed and returned the stubs to the ashtray.

"Well, what!" he yelled, cleaning the ash from the carpet and making it even dirtier.

She watched the process of his self-exposure in excitement; a spectacle no less rare in him than demonstrations of love.

"If you've got something to say, say it."

"Never mind, you'll hear it yourself soon enough."

"Do you want to annoy me?"

Yes, she didn't say, I very much want to annoy you. Instead, she smiled sadly.

"What, Ruth," he said, a note of supplication beginning to show in his voice.

"There's talk that they're not going to renew your appointment at the university in September."

"What?"

"There's talk that... you're going to be dismissed."

"Talk by who?"

"People are talking, Robert. Times are hard."

The veins on his neck swelled and the blood rose in his face. The remains of the mask dropped and left it frightened and confused. As soon as he recovered he made haste to look for someone to blame. "I can imagine who spread those rumors, the reactionary establishment windbags. A bunch of old degenerates who can't stand the presence of an independent-minded young person among them."

"They're firing Jews, Robert. You needn't take it personally."

"And why are you so happy," he brandished his hand which remained arrested in midair, suspended embarrassingly between heaven and earth, "I feel like hitting you."

"Look at you, Robert," she said lightly, "I didn't think you would take it so hard. I even thought it would come as a certain relief. You've told me more than once that working on nuclear physics is in conflict with your moral code."

His brain began to work again. He put on his boots and rushed towards the door.

"I didn't mean it. Nobody's firing you."

He turned round slowly, looking at her in astonishment, taking it in. She stood with her back to the window, her arms crossed, a thin crack of a smile jubilant on her face. "I suddenly felt like getting to know the man I love so much in depth. Like everyone else. Inside there's an ugly frightened animal. After that scene I love you a tiny bit less."

He took off his boots and lay down on the bed with his eyes closed. She would be punished.

"I'm sorry," she said and began to reproach herself. The punishment was out of proportion to the crime. What did he say, after all? But it wasn't what he said, it was the way he had greeted her daughter.

When he opened the door and saw that she had been obliged to bring the child with her again, he was horrified, as if he had just received news of a catastrophe. And it wasn't that she was insulted for her daughter's sake, she hadn't even thought about her yet. What had provoked the insult was his demonstration of revulsion with regard to her motherhood, to her life that wasn't connected to him, a further proof of the unreasonableness of the fantasy of a life together which she diligently cultivated in her husband's bed.

"Enough, Robert, I'm sorry. We've played crueler games before."

He went on sulking with his eyes closed.

"I'm sorry. Stop it. Talk to me."

"I'm bored," he said at last. "I'm simply bored. And I'm hungry," he added in order to demonstrate business as usual.

"What are you bored with?"

"I don't know, apparently with you. Go away Ruth, I want to sleep."

"Robert," she whispered, in a voice that whistled like a dying respirator. "What's happening to us."

"Nothing," he replied, dry as ice, "we're rotting away."

Translated from the Hebrew by Dalya Bilu

ALONA FRANKEL was born in 1937 in Cracow, Poland, and spent her childhood during World War II in the Lvov ghetto, then in hiding— first alone, later with her parents. After immigrating to Israel with her family in 1949, Frankel studied art at the Avni Institute. She began illustrating children's books at the age of 30. In 1975, she published the first of the 31 children's books that she both wrote and illustrated, in addition to illustrating dozens of books by other children's authors. Her books, translated into 12 languages, have become bestsellers. She lectures on illustration at several institutions, and her work has been featured at exhibitions and fairs in Israel and abroad. Frankel has won numerous prizes, including an Andersen Honor Citation. *A Girl*, her first book for adults, was awarded the prestigious Sapir Prize in 2005.

A Girl

Tel Aviv, Mapa, 2004. 280 pp.

Alona Frankel

A Girl

I t was night, and in the little room where we were staying in
the ghetto, there were four of us: my mother, my father, I and the
strange woman. This is Hanya Seremet, my mother told me. Ilusyu,
Kochanye, she said, from now on your name is Irena Seremet.

An excerpt from the novel

Not Ilona, not Ilka, not Ilonka, not Ilusya. From now on you
are I-re-na Se-re-met. Irena Seremet, for-e-ver. Irena. And my mother
went on to say:

> Our Father which art in heaven, hallowed be thy name,
> Thy kingdom come, thy will be done,
> On earth as it is in heaven.
> Give us this day our daily bread,
> And forgive us our sins,
> As we forgive those who sin against us,
> And do not lead us into temptation,
> But deliver us from evil.

> Repeat it after me, my mother said.
> I repeated it.

Again, she said.

I repeated it again.

And again.

I said it for the third time.

My father stood at the window looking out into the night, his back to me.

I already knew the words, and in the right order.

And now kneel down, my mother said, you have to go down on your knees and put your hands together. Like this.

My mother leaned over me and arranged my limbs, like arranging a doll.

Bend your head down, my mother said.

Now once more, for the last time, say it again.

Our Father which art in heaven, hallowed be thy name…

I didn't make a single mistake.

I opened my eyes for a moment, kneeling with head bent over my joined hands, and with a quick sidelong glance caught the satisfied expression on my mother's face. She looked at Hanya Seremet as if saying: Well, didn't I tell you? I promised you the girl would learn, and learn quickly! I know my daughter.

My mother and my father already knew Hanya Seremet. They cut a deal with her: such and such a sum of money in exchange for my life.

Apparently Hanya Seremet had cast doubt on the ability of a little girl like me to learn the Lord's Prayer so quickly. A nice prayer. To me it was just words and sounds.

Everything was so hurried.

I believed the world was like this.

What was I thinking to myself? Was I thinking?

I stood up from my kneeling position. Hanya Seremet took from my mother some papers and a bundle. Later I discovered that the bundle contained some ragged clothes of mine, including the wine-colored velvet dress with the lace collar and the white trimmings.

I put on my only pair of shoes.

The papers were my forged documents. Apparently they had been prepared some time in advance, and a lot of money had been paid for them. Hanya Seremet definitely received a lot of money too, with the promise of more and more in the future, in exchange for taking me out of the ghetto which was on the verge of destruction, and hiding me in a village with her parents, as a Christian girl with a Christian name.

My mother and father didn't tell me anything about the strange woman who was going to come and take me in the middle of the night to a strange place.

The deal had been made.

And what did I think, what did I feel?

A girl.

The four of us: my mother, my father, Hanya Seremet and I went out to the dark, short and narrow corridor. From the rooms on both sides wafted an odor of deep sleep, the rustle of dreams and momentary release from fear.

Before the door, again the vile stench, bad enough to make your eyes water. The communal toilet. Last door on the right.

A stinking toilet, dark and dirty: the bowl broken, glass shattered, and what was once white had turned brown. There was no seat, and my fear of falling into the filthy black hole was such that I held on tight to the rim of the cracked bowl, however disgusted it made me feel. The smell, or the memory of the smell, stuck to my hands and followed me around everywhere.

High up, under the ceiling, hung the cast-iron cistern. Its paint was flaking off too. Some kind of symbol was embossed on it, a shape and some writing in an oval script, but for all my staring at it, and all my efforts to understand it, I never succeeded in working out what it was.

All kinds of things were attached to the handle of the flush: string, the end of a chain, electric cable, bits of a belt. Time and again these extensions were ripped out of place by energetic pulling and a new one had to be improvised—always hung beyond my reach.

From the leprous walls, with their covering of oil paint, colored olive-green, layers of paint and plaster had peeled and in some places the bricks were exposed. The walls were mottled not only by the amalgam of oil paint, plaster and brickwork, but by brown smears running in various directions. Between the layers of peeling plaster and the brown smears it was very easy to make out animals, people, towers, monsters and flowers—marvelous and curious shapes.

My father opened the outer door. We went out, and down the wooden stairs. The creaking stair creaked, the iron rail was damp and cold.

For a long time the smell of the iron rail stuck to my hand. This smell had a heavy taste to it, dark and pungent. When we lived in Cracow and there was no war in the world, the frozen brass poles of the trams had a similar taste.

We went out into the street.

Behind us layers of old smells remained, the stench of cabbage and vile pig-fat.

I tried not to breathe.

You can block your ears, you can close your eyes.

Very difficult not to breathe.

We went out.

The odors of the poverty diet trailed behind us.

It was a humid night full of air.

I breathed.

We walked hurriedly in a straight line, close to the walls of houses. The further we went from the apartment we lived in, the lower the houses were.

No one held my hand.

We hurried.

Hanya Seremet, I, my mother, my father, and a great horde of rats, some small and some huge, making our escape.

Rats were escaping in the opposite direction too.

The night was dark and from far away, apparently from the direction of the guard-towers on the edge of the ghetto, came the sounds of laughter, and long beams of light probed the neighborhood. I didn't cry.

We reached a place that was perhaps the end of the ghetto. A simple fence, nothing impressive about it.

I didn't cry.

We stopped, Hanya Seremet, I, my mother and father. No one held my hand.

I didn't cry.

Hanya Seremet pushed me through a gap in the fence to the other side and squeezed through after me.

I didn't cry.

I didn't turn my head.

I was abandoned.

My mother told me, told me and told me again about the way back to the ghetto. How I hated all those stories.

She told me how she had wept and wept and wept.

After Hanya Seremet took me.

After I was abandoned.

She told me what a difficult journey it had been back to the ghetto, hobbling along, leaning on my father.

My father never told me anything.

So we handed you over, my mother said. To Hanya Seremet we handed you over, to almost certain death. To Hanya Seremet, the murderess.

When we handed you over to that murderess, my mother said, I wept all the way back. It was like coming home from a funeral, from my daughter's funeral, my only daughter. I didn't believe I'd ever see you again.

So my mother told me.

I so much hated hearing her talk about that night, about the way back.

Many years later, a great many years later, I asked my mother: Mamusyu, tell me please—I always addressed my mother in the formal style, and I never raised my voice or used a word not considered nice—why did you hand me over to that woman, that Hanya Seremet, if you thought you were handing me over to certain death?

But Kochanye, we had no other choice, there was no other way out, my mother answered my question impatiently, expressing surprise that I didn't understand the situation: Hanya Seremet was the only one who agreed to take you. We already had a hiding-place sorted out with Yuzak in Panyenska Street, but they weren't prepared under any circumstances to take a child!

There was no choice.

We were all lost.

It's absolutely clear.

And this was after all the events, just before the final liquidation of the ghetto, the last moment!

To the Little Girl

I want to tell you a story,
My little girl,
The girl that I was,
The girl that I am,
The girl that's inside me.
I stretch out my arms to you.
Come.
Ilona, Ilka, Ilonka, Ilusya.
My little one.
I gather you in my arms.
I embrace you.
I clutch you to my body.
You're inside me.
You were a girl, as was I.
My two sons were born of you, of me.
They were in you, in me,
And in them are my grandchildren and great-grandchildren
to come.
I stretch out my arms to you,
Girl,
Come.
I take you in my arms,
I want to embrace you,
To watch over you,
To be with you,
To look at you,

To listen to you.
To touch you,
To protect you,
To console you,
You
You
You
I want to caress your head,
Your hair,
Your face,
Until the end of time,
And lull you to sleep in my arms
With warmth and compassion.
I have wrapped you up in safety,
Little girl,
In my arms,
In me.
My comfort is in you
Do not worry! Do not worry! Do not worry!
I won't abandon you ever,
I won't abandon you as long as I live,
Since we shall die together,
You and I.
I want to tell you a story
Of what used to be in the past.
Of what I remember of the past.
I want to tell you a story.
And I will weep
And you too will weep,
Weep without worry,
Weep without hiding anything
It's a good ending.
So be it.

The thin and tall Hanya Seremet, with the skin of her face
stretched white and shiny over high cheekbones, and her jaws square

and sealed shut, her flashing green eyes and hair, lashes and brows blacker than black, mouth as narrow as a well-healed wound, the lovely and the elegant Hanya Seremet was a criminal.

A murderess, exactly as my mother dubbed her.

She was well-known in the ghetto.

She had good connections. She had dealings with the Germans and the Gestapo. She made a lot of deals. There were many Jews in the ghetto whom she promised to help, finding them hiding-places on the Aryan side. She used to take them out, whole families, the richer ones, only the rich, with their diamonds, their furs, their money, their ornaments, with the forged papers that cost a fortune, with promises and hopes for a refuge, for a future, for life. Many of these people were thrown back into the ghetto, penniless. The fate of the others was unknown.

My mother told me, told me again and again.

Only she was prepared to take me. In exchange for money, of course, and not a small sum of money.

That was a lie, the money.

My mother and father lied to Hanya Seremet about the money.

There was no money. There was a little money, very little. Certainly not the fortune they had promised Hanya Seremet. My father filled his warehouses with goods just before the German invasion.

My father never owed anything to anyone. My father paid cash for all the merchandise he bought. His warehouses were bursting with building materials while all around the destruction of everything had begun, and we, my mother, my father and I escaped with one suitcase and no money.

All was lost, as the gypsy prophesied.

Hanya Seremet, the murderess, handed people over to their deaths.

But not always. Not all of them.

Me, for example, she didn't hand over.

We passed through the fence, Hanya Seremet and I, just the two of us.

We were out of the ghetto, on the Aryan side, the side of life.

Suddenly there were no rats. Stretching out before us was an enormous open space. A square? An empty lot? At the end of it stood a triangular corner-house, with two streets running parallel to its flanks.

We started walking, the strange woman Hanya Seremet, the woman I had seen for the first time that evening, and I. We went up on the pavement. Very tall trees grew on both sides. The streets were very broad. There were no rats. A dog stood there. The road was paved with the oval stones known as cats' heads.

The carriage had rattled over cats' heads like these, taking my mother and father to the exclusive maternity hospital in Cracow to await my birth. And in a puddle in an enclosed yard in Lvov paved with cats' heads like these, I had found my precious dead rat. The night was damp, and from time to time the tram-tracks gleamed with a blue luster. It was impressive.

The dog that stood there suddenly started moving. The direction of its stooping gait was the only way of telling which end was the head and which was the tail.

The night was growing lighter, darkness fading.

A man with head bowed between hunched shoulders, collar turned up and hands dug deep in his pockets, passed by in the opposite direction to that taken by the dog. A thin trickle began, of people and rain. A tram with two carriages passed with a pulsating din—wheels grinding and lightning flashes from the electric cables.

Nice and happy sounds.

Sparks flew from the tracks, like fireworks. The lit windows of the carriages were empty. Only at three of them were silhouettes visible, passengers wrapped up in themselves. In the first carriage stood the conductor.

Afterwards, when the war is over, if I'm still alive and the Germans haven't succeeded in murdering me, how I would love to stand behind the conductor admiringly and watch his deft and precise movements as he plays a tune on the handles, the tubes, the dials, the magnificent acceleration and braking mechanisms with their trimmings of burnished brass.

The night grew lighter still.

The wind that had risen brought with it smells of a horse, straw, sour milk and the drowsy weariness of people. A train whistle was heard, not far away, an innocent sound. Still innocent then. The dairy cart passed by us, and a white and warm smell passed with it.

The music of the horse's hooves, the clatter of cartwheels on the cats' heads, the full tin vessels clanging together and the splashing of the milk in the churns. The figure of the driver, the dairyman, head buried between his shoulders like the dog, like the passer-by, like the passengers in the tram.

The strange, thin and tall woman named Hanya Seremet and I reached the railway station. It was no longer night.

In the carriage we traveled in, Hanya Seremet and I, there were a lot of soldiers too. German soldiers. They had already been there some time when we boarded the train.

They were handsome and clean. The smell that wafted from them was the woolen fabric of their uniforms, boot polish and soap. They were friendly and cheerful. They flirted gallantly with Hanya Seremet and played with me.

They gave me cubes of sugar. They said I was as pretty as a doll.

I remember that.

Hanya Semeret wrote proudly to my mother, telling how I had captivated the hearts of the Wehrmacht with my beauty and charm.

My mother repeated this story endlessly, told it, told it and told it.

How I hated all these stories.

I always felt some guilt, and I was repelled by the importance my mother attached to compliments from German soldiers.

The train traveled on, not for long. Rain was no longer falling and the sky was clearing. A fine day.

We reached the village, a tiny station. We climbed up on the dust road and walked, the strange woman who carried the bundle with my ragged clothing, my forged papers, her shiny black briefcase—and I.

I didn't cry.

She didn't hold my hand.

I went on not crying.

It seems I believed the world was like this.

We walked on the dust road, we arrived.

The name of the village was Marchinkovitze. The tall and strange Polish woman Hanya Semeret and I arrived in the village of her birth, at her parents' home. Or perhaps it was the home of her grandfather and grandmother, I don't know. What do I remember? What do I really remember? And maybe I'm remembering a story someone told me? And maybe it's a story I thought up in my head? And maybe I just dreamt it?

The smell that I remember is real.

You can't make up a smell.

Translated from the Hebrew by Philip Simpson

DAN TSALKA (1936–2005) was born in Warsaw, Poland, and spent many years during World War II in Siberia and Kazakhstan. In 1946, he returned to Poland where he studied philosophy and literature. He immigrated to Israel in 1957, continued his studies, and later went to Grenoble, France to study the manuscripts of Stendhal.

Tsalka taught at Tel Aviv University, at Ben Gurion University, and was writer-in-residence at the Hebrew University of Jerusalem. He was also literary advisor to the Players' Stage Theater, and editor of the literary review *Masa*, as well as an art magazine. Tsalka published six novels, eight collections of short stories, three books of poetry, three books of essays, an autobiography, and three children's books. He received several awards, including the Brenner Prize (1976), the Alterman Prize (1992), the ACUM Prize twice (1994, 2000) and the Sapir Prize for *Tsalka's ABC* (2004). His work has been translated into six languages. *Tsalka's ABC* will soon be appearing in Spanish.

Tsalka's ABC
Tel Aviv, Xargol, 2003. 178 pp.

Dan Tsalka

Tsalka's ABC

Vignettes of a Life

Beauties

Meeting a real beauty was always a cause of upheaval and shock for me because apart from the obvious excitement that gripped me, I was dazzled. Before I met Megan, a model working in Paris who was not a perfect beauty (although in her photographs she was without blemish), I'd known two beauties. After the dazzle, the paralysis, the unnatural behavior and the inevitable idolization, nothing of the hoped-for mystery took place. Or to be more precise: it did, but in the same mystifying way that things between women and men always happen, with or without great beauty.

Due to chance travel circumstances, I slept in a bed with the first beauty after we'd agreed that an invisible sword would separate our bodies. I, of course, lay with my eyes wide open in the dark, hoping the sentence would be commuted, until I finally dropped off. So I was amazed when long, slow caresses woke me up and a warm, naked body cuddled up to me. But the following evening, the beauty's friend told me what she had told her, and I didn't like what I heard. The beauty was very puzzled by the secrets of sex: she had

107

never thought of me as a lover—far from it—and now after being next to me in bed…

Far from it? The insult was boundless! The fact that her story wasn't accurate and that she'd concealed the fact that we'd only gone to sleep at noon deepened the hurt.

The second beauty sensed my shock and treated me with charm and simplicity. We climbed a high mountain and slept side by side in sleeping bags in a chalet. It was nice sleeping next to her, imprisoned in a sleeping bag. The scent of her hair was particularly delightful.

Megan. Not a real beauty? What I mean is that there was something ostentatious and perhaps petty in her face, like with many actresses. Her previous boyfriend was still around. He was drunk most of the time, not particularly clean, and he smoked (vigorously) a lot of Sweet Caporal cigarettes. They'd broken off their relationship, but because of their relatively long history I suspected—perhaps not without cause—that sometimes (infrequently) it was renewed. And there was someone else, the forty-seven-year-old French gentleman with hawk eyes and beautifully done hair, who drove a black car and came to take Megan away for weekends. Megan brushed away my complaints with denial: soft and smiling about her former boyfriend, hard and dry about the owner of the black car.

She was a beauty. I stared at her for ages as she combed her hair and painted her nails. Our walks were not completely relaxed. Conceit and pride—yes, but also a fear that somebody would steal my treasure. Not that we went out a lot. Makeup, fittings and photo shoots take a great deal of time. But there were other things that aroused doubts, anguish, the shakes. One day I felt a worrying itch. I went to a pharmacy and after much hesitation asked for a suitable powder. Afterwards, my shins were suddenly covered with pink blotches. It was odd, because Megan herself didn't suffer from any illness or infection. Her body was always perfect, clear and white.

Although these symptoms were unpleasant, there was something else that made me shudder. Megan used to pass out. At first I saw these faints as a compliment to my virility and qualities as a lover, because they usually happened after particularly tempestuous episodes, but slowly they began to frighten me. The only thing I remembered from my teens was that after an especially strong orgasm I'd sink into sleep, although I'd wake up again far too quickly. I fully recall those moments of falling asleep—the knife-blade sharpness—but they were nothing like Megan's fainting. It scared me so much I'd put my head against her chest to listen to her heartbeat, and touch an artery or the pulse in the wrist, the way years later I checked my baby son when he was too quiet in his crib.

She asked me to move in with her for a while. I didn't take my things from my room in Rue des Carmes, but I did take a bag with a few essentials. Some time later, she went away for the weekend with the owner of the black car, but untypically she didn't return on the Monday. Four days passed, then five, and six. I knew she hadn't called because I was in the apartment most of the time, drinking wine and writing a bizarre morality play. I think that in spite of everything, I'd somehow believed her denials, and so her extended stay in the south was a blow. I told myself that if she hadn't had an accident or fallen sick, I'd leave her. I thought she'd asked me to live with her as a sort of last line of defense. She came back two weeks later, and we parted after a terrible quarrel. I also parted from the ideal of "the beauty" and from the ability to live an adventurous love story with by Rossini-like schemes.

I heard about Megan by chance from a barman in an Edinburgh pub. All's well that ends well. Behind the barman there hung a photograph of a woman—an angel on a red horse—who might have been taken from the Book of Zechariah. Her hair was long and ginger (possibly natural), and she was fuller.

"Megan!" I said, amazed.

"Did you know Megan?"

Fate had smiled on her. I raised my whiskey glass, and invited the barman to have one, too. We drank Megan's health.

Lightning

A bolt of lightning—suddenly falling in love. With an animal, an object, a city, even an artist. In a museum in Verona, I saw a small greenish Madonna that captivated me on the spot. How could I tear my eyes away from her? Look at other paintings? Leave the hall? The museum? I memorized the artist's name: Carlo Crivelli. I traveled north. In Milan's Pinacoteca di Brera I recognized his technique and his style. I stood before *The Coronation of the Virgin* for about half an hour. It was as if the artist had knelt before the Madonna, pitying, adoring, giving himself to her in painful and sublime idealism.

At the National Gallery in London, his *Demidoff Altarpiece* dazzled me. I know this may sound strange, because a painting isn't a story or a piece of music that exists in time, but I'm sure that in the fraction of a second it took my eyes to see the wings of the herald angel, I guessed the exact tint in which they would end.

London's an easy city for finding books. I began reading up on Crivelli, a Venetian painter who—because of some crime or other mystery—left his city and moved to Ancona and Ascoli. There was very little material on him. The years of his birth and death are unknown. A few articles from the end of the nineteenth century, a mediocre monograph, a few sentences in Berenson (he of the eye that sees and the intellect that understands the artist's soul), but they were too incidental and didn't trace Crivelli's unique combinations. I liked the words he used to compare the luster of Crivelli's works with Japanese lacquer. Actually, nothing worthwhile had been written about the artist.

In Rome I decided to write a book about him, without giving much thought to the fact that anyone who isn't an art historian or part of a respected circle, who isn't a university don, doesn't belong to a research institute, and has no private means, would do better to write stories in a notebook (I wrote *Bassoon Wood* back then), and give up his pretensions to a project of that sort.

It was clear to me that love demands enormous effort and costs a great deal. But I was in love.

I'm not a suspicious man, but I became rather wary when faced with the reticence of the professionals I met. Perhaps unjustifiably. Truth is, they gave me some sound advice and were even friendly about it, but the advice was given in such a way that an ignorant outsider like myself couldn't always guess its usefulness, so much of my research ended up a blind alley.

But still, I slowly got to see Crivelli's paintings. I didn't have the money to go to Berlin and several other places, but I found some good slides and photographs. Then a new problem emerged: some of the paintings were being restored and were kept in various odd places. There were even two in Rome itself, at the Castel Sant'Angelo. I asked to see them and even learnt to tip the attendants, but I didn't know how to look at paintings leaning against a wall surrounded by ladders and plastic sheets, tables loaded with rolls of paper and small bottles. It was only years later that I managed to "become intimate" with a painting and commune with it in such a state. Bellini's legendary *Feast of the Gods* was being restored at the National Gallery of Art in Washington (we now know that both Titian's and Dosso Dossi's hands were in the painting). They let me go upstairs and see it. I was escorted by a guard, a hugely fat man with a big pistol in his belt. It was a gray, dark wintry day. I sat down in front of the painting in an empty hall with many tall windows. The guard leant against a wall. I almost sank into its beauty, and then I heard stentorian snoring: the guard had fallen asleep standing up. I went to wake him gently (a pistol's a pistol), but his own snores woke him up. And wonder of wonders—I still managed to see the painting. Later, I also went to restoration workshops in Milan, and the sanctum sanctorum of Italian restoration, the Fortezza in Florence. I enjoyed those mainly because of the condition of the paintings.

In any event, the box where I kept the material on Crivelli gradually filled up.

The first sign of something wrong—a crack that was likely to widen—appeared when I went to Ancona. There was a Crivelli triptych in the church of Massa Fermana, a small walled village. I traveled to Porto San Giorgio, a modest and somewhat remote holiday resort, and from there I took a taxi to Massa Fermana. It was a rainy, windy day. Although the fare had been agreed on in advance, I was worried that the driver would ask for more: a tree had fallen onto the road, there was a cloudburst right ahead of us. I only had a few miserable bills in my pocket. Finding the church wasn't difficult. It was closed. I rang the verger's doorbell. Nobody answered. I went back to the church. A light push opened a side door: the church looked abandoned and wretched, and a couple of windows were banging in the strong wind. One glance, and I knew—there was no triptych there. Meanwhile two old men appeared: the triptych was being restored.

Although it was still early, it was very dark in Porto San Giorgio when we got back. Through the windows I saw a well-lit hotel lobby. It was crowded with dozens of people in evening dress. Another group was nearer the entrance. Luckily, I heard that a tour bus was leaving for Rome in fifteen minutes. I went outside and gave the driver my remaining money. The trip to Massa Fermana, the two old men, and especially the sight of the empty, neglected church where all I could hear was the whistling wind—all that came back to me and depressed me a little. Earlier, when I'd read how the young Berenson had trudged from one remote church to another in search of paintings, it had seemed intriguing and adventurous. Why, then, this strange depression? Fatigue? Doubt? I thought about the short visit to Massa Fermana like a man recalling an accident from which he'd barely escaped unhurt.

Before returning to Tel Aviv, I took a good look at my material on Crivelli. The most important part, the descriptions of the paintings, seemed good. Between the serious and the playful, Gothic echoes and youthfulness, the originality of his decorations and his provincial faith, the image of the artist began to emerge. For the most part, the history of the paintings was extremely detailed and quite sufficient for someone who, like me, was not very demanding. My Roman friends told me that in a year or two some books on Crivelli were going to be published and that the catalogues in them would draw attention.

A bolt of lightning? Woe to lovers! Only a few months passed and the thought of writing the book became a burden. I began to discuss it with various people, something I never do before I finish writing. *Bassoon Wood* had been published. So that was when I should have started. But instead of sitting down to it, I put the box in the wardrobe, and later moved it next to the boiler. It was an expulsion. The amazing Crivelli lived inside the box; a year later—he vanished.

Translated from the Hebrew by Anthony Berris

Born in Haifa in 1963, JUDITH KATZIR studied literature and cinema at Tel Aviv University. At present, she works as an editor for Hakibbutz Hameuchad/Siman Kriah Publishing House and teaches creative writing. Katzir, a bestselling author in Israel, has published two collections of stories and novellas, two novels and two children's books. Her books have been translated into nine languages. In addition to literary prizes for individual stories, Katzir has received the Book Publishers' Association's Platinum and Gold Book Prizes, the Prime Minister's Prize (1996), and the French WIZO Prize for *Matisse Has the Sun in His Belly* (2004). Her books have been translated into nine languages. *Dearest Anne* will be published in German, French and Turkish translation.

Dearest Anne (previously *Here I Begin*)

Tel Aviv, Hakibbutz Hameuchad / Siman Kriah, 2003. 304 pp.

Judith Katzir

Dearest Anne

An excerpt from the novel

FRIDAY, 8.9.78

Dearest Anne,

"In a peaceful little town between mountain and sea, there once lived a young woman and a girl, who loved each other terribly, even though it was forbidden." If I ever find the courage in years to come to write our story, this will be the opening sentence. Perhaps I'll call the story "Love between mountain and sea," what do you think? Michaela is the mountain, my magic mountain ('Berg' means mountain in German, as you know), her warm brown eyes are the earth and the tree trunks, and I am the sea, which is blue-gray like my eyes, and stormy like my soul. The mountain slides into the sea and the sea laps the mountain. The sea loves the mountain and the mountain loves the sea. They succeed in touching each other.

The school year has begun, and I'm writing to you in my new notebook, with its coffee-colored cover, that Michaela brought me for London. Every now and then I raise it to my nose and breathe, and try not to think that it was once a cow peacefully chewing the cud in some English meadow.

Michaela isn't teaching us this year. She had planned to complete her thesis on Lea Goldberg by the end of summer and receive her MA, which is a condition for teaching the top grades in our school; but she neglected the thesis and failed to complete it, and so she has to go on teaching in the middle school. Strange to think that I've gone up to high school, and she has remained behind, but I think that it's a relief for both of us, because at the end of last year it was getting harder and harder for us to pretend and act the parts of teacher and pupil, when all the time we knew that straight after class we were going to fly on the wings of Rocinanta to the forest. You can imagine the picture: me with my chin and cheek resting on my hand, my eyes half-shut, watching her supple body moving along the blackboard, and Michaela sending me looks after every brilliant remark, to see if I'm scratching my forehead or my nose, and occasionally getting confused and closing her eyes and holding her temples with her thumb and finger, and saying, can anyone remind me where we were, and some Michal or Anat hurries to tie the thread of her thought for her. You must remember how once, after we quarreled, I sat opposite her with a sour face, and Michaela gave the lesson in total absent-mindedness and looked as if she was going to burst into tears at any moment. Towards the end of the year, we were so afraid of giving ourselves away, that we decided I should stop putting my hand up and taking part in the lesson, and Michaela complained that she wasn't enjoying herself any more because she had nobody to talk to. This year our literature and expression teacher is someone called Nira, who is also our homeroom teacher. She has tiny brown eyes and thin black hair and skin that looks like dough pricked with a fork, and a sack like a toad's hanging from her neck, and I feel a little sorry for her, because she always looks tired. At eight o'clock in the morning she's already tired. She recites passages from the textbook, and I miss Michaela's warmth and vivacity, her enthusiasm for a well-written sentence, a description, an image, her way of finding connections between details that seem random, and showing how every detail echoes another. She's supposed to give birth at the end of March or the beginning of April, and after her maternity leave it will already be the long vacation, and she won't be coming back to school until next year.

Yesterday after class she picked me up in Rocinanta, as usual, and we drove up the hill almost as far as Kibbutz Beit-Oren, and found ourselves a padded bed between the pines. I laid my head on her stomach and we rested together like two naked nymphs in a forest. Michaela's body hasn't changed yet, her stomach is still flat, only her breasts are fuller and rounder, and the haloes round her nipples are darker, the first hint of what is to come. I told her that in three years time, when I'm eighteen, I'll want us to move in together, with the baby, and we'll have to have the necessary courage—she to tell Yoel and her parents, and me to tell my mother. I told her that I would always love her, and that our love is far greater and stronger than anything people will think and say about us. We could go and live together in Tel Aviv, in a house next to the sea, she could work as a teacher and go on studying at the university, and I would find a way to get out of the army, I would work as a waitress, and start studying literature or cinema. Michaela rumpled my hair and said quietly, that she couldn't think that far ahead, in the meantime she couldn't even imagine what it would be like to be a mother. Three years were a long time, especially at my age, and my dreams might change and grow with me. I stood on my knees, naked, only my hair loose on my back—she always undoes my braids when we make love—and took hold of both her hands and asked, but do you want to live with me? Just tell me if you want to.

Michaela smiled a tired, rather sad smile, and said, "Of course I want to, my kitten, I'd like to live with you all the time, to go to sleep with you and dream with you and wake up with you, and perhaps in three years time we'll live in a little house next to the sea, like Charlie Chaplin and his wife in *Modern Times*, I'll go out to work in the morning, and you'll wave a white handkerchief at me."

"You don't believe it," I said, trying not to cry, "you don't believe in us at all."

"I believe in the need to observe the commandments of life," she said quietly, "your love gives me the strength to get up every morning and go to teach gladly, and I would like my love to give you too the strength to study and write and develop."

I really have been writing a lot recently, as in a kind of fever, almost every week I write two or three poems, as if my body can't contain all my love any more and it brims over like boiling milk, and I told Michaela that she was my private Muse. (I've discovered that the desire for a body and the desire to write stem from the same source). But I haven't got the strength to study, especially the new and irritating subjects like physics and chemistry. Luckily these lessons are at the end of the day, and I try my best to escape them in order to meet Michaela. I feel the need to be with her as much as possible, because after she gives birth—who knows if we'll be able to go on the way we are now.

We've been together now for almost a year, would you believe it?

Your Kitty.

P.S. I almost forgot to tell you—in honor of the pregnancy Michaela has stopped smoking! Completely! It wasn't hard for her to quit, because the taste and smell of the cigarettes make her nauseous. I'm so pleased. Yesterday I told her that her kisses taste much better now, they no longer taste like an ashtray.

Sukkoth holidays

Dearest Anne,

Michaela's parents have gone to the guest house at Kiryat-Anavim (it turns out that for years they've been booking holidays in Israel and also flights abroad through Grandfather's travel agency...). This afternoon I drove with her to their house in the suburb of Carmelia to take their mail out of the mailbox and water the garden and the potted plants. The house looks more or less as I imagined it; dark heavy furniture and thick carpets, and the walls covered with paintings by German and Israeli artists, Marcel Janko and Nahum Gutman and Manya Katz and others, who exhibited at Michaela's father's gallery, and some of them became friendly with him and gave him paintings as presents, with personal dedications on the back.

Her childhood room has hardly changed; on the shelves the big volumes of "Art" and "Civilization" whose pages Michaela would turn and imagine that she was strolling in gorgeous dresses between the statues and the paintings and riding in carriages with velvet curtains. From the top shelf the china dolls her father brought her from his trips to England looked down at us, in all their wealth of costumes and hairdos and bonnets and parasols.

On the bottom shelf I discovered a photograph album from her childhood and I fell on it delightedly. We sat on the veranda open to the garden and breathed in the white scent of the jasmine which ran riot over the wall. (I reminded Michaela that she had spoken about jasmine in our first lesson in the eighth grade, when she read us Lea Goldberg's poem, and her voice poured into me dark and dense as honey, and I couldn't stop looking at her. Only two years have passed since then, and it seems so long ago…). Michaela opened the sprinkler, which clicked and nodded its head, spitting water onto the lawn fainting in the heat, and on our feet.

We drank lemonade with fresh mint from the garden, and looked at the jagged-edged black-and-white photos, stuck with little transparent triangles to the black cardboard pages. Here is my beloved at the age of four or five, a slender child in a white dress, with a ribbon in her hair, pushing a doll in a toy baby-carriage, her big eyes wide in surprise at the world and its wonders. And here she is in a dress with puffed sleeves and patent leather shoes, in the garden of the Ritz Café with her parents, who look young and smiling, her mother glamorous as an old movie star in a pleated bell skirt and high-heeled shoes, and her father in a light three-piece suit and fancy summer shoes with holes punched in them, and the child Michaela smiling without front teeth behind a stainless steel goblet with three scoops of ice cream and a triangular wafer. And here she's already older, nine or ten, in short pants and boots, with a round cloth hat on her head, standing hand in hand with her beloved aunt, a lean tanned German Jewess with short gray hair, hiking in the Jerusalem hills. And here she is at twelve, on the beach with her best friend Osnat—a lanky girl with a mane of curls and light laughing eyes—both of them flat-chested, in bikinis with the bottoms coming up to their navels, and

Michaela's freckles are so prominent they look as if they're about to jump right out of the picture. And here she is sitting next to a pale blond boy with matchstick legs, in a decorated carriage drawn by a white horse, and I recognize him and almost shout "It's Yoel!" And Michaela smiles and says, "Yes, once we went with our parents to a guest-house in Nahariya. One night we walked along the beach and I tried to persuade him to swim in the nude, but he was too scared. He was already a Yoram then."

After I'd finished going thoroughly through the album, I took a few folded pages with new poems on them out of my pocket, and also the beginning of a story about a student at an art class who falls in love with the nude model, and I read it aloud to her: "In the room there were a lot of people. Quiet, each absorbed in his canvas. It was very cold outside. They were wearing sweaters but their fingers holding the paintbrushes were frozen and stiff. In one corner there was a small electric heater, and opposite its two blazing red bars lay the model, on her side, the front of her body and her face turned to the painters, and her crooked arm partly hiding her heavy breasts. He allowed her pale nakedness to seep into him through the cigarette smoke. The smell of orange peel reached his nostrils and mingled with the smell of the oil paints raging to escape their swollen tubes and create new revolutions.

"He looked at the blank canvas, ran his fingers over it, dipped his brush in the red paint and began to give shape to the woman's curls swarming with life."

Michaela laughed at the oil paints raging to escape their swollen tubes (I swear I didn't notice...), and then she said quietly, "One day you'll have to start taking your talent seriously."

"Why do you say that," I was offended, and Michaela said that I was too in love with words, with the glories of language, and sometimes the words took charge of me instead of me taking charge of them. My writing would recover from childhood diseases only when I renounced grand words and learned the secret of economy.

"It seems to me that every poem I write is the last one, and I have to put everything into it, like a suicide note," I tried to explain to her, and to myself as well.

"You'll have many more years in which to write many more poems and stories, so why don't you forget about the suicide notes, and try to write a love letter," she smiled at me with narrowed eyes.

"And the story? The first lines wrote themselves, but suddenly I got writer's block, and I couldn't go on."

"Nothing that's any good writes itself," she picked a jasmine flower and crushed it between her fingers, "and writer's block is another word for laziness. The only cure is work. You have to sit and write a few hours every day, you have to regard it as a job, as work, not something you only do when you're in the mood, even if it means sitting like a dummy in front of a blank page—in the end something will emerge. You have keep at it day after day after day. And in the end you have to organize, rewrite and polish. Someone once said that talent is only ten percent, and all the rest is perseverance. Your talent is a rare and wonderful gift, but only if you treat it with respect will it open the world before you."

"And what about inspiration? You yourself once wrote me something about the muses."

"The muses are demanding and pampered goddesses," she reached for my hand over the table and held it, "when they see that someone is working really hard, they appear in his room, sit on his shoulder, and whisper one or two good lines into his ear."

What do you think, Anne? Can you see my backside stuck to a chair with carpenter's glue for hours on end, day after day? Do you think I'll ever succeed in writing good poems and stories that people will actually buy in bookstores and read and be moved?

Your Kitty

P.S. Today I forgot to phone Racheli as usual before I went home to ask if my mother had been checking up on me. When I got home she asked me where I had been, and I told her I'd gone to visit Racheli. She said she'd called Racheli's house and I wasn't there. On the spot I invented a complicated story about how I'd gone round to Racheli's and she wasn't there, and then by chance in the street, I met another girl from our class who lives next door to her, and she invited me to her place... Mother studied me suspiciously for a moment, but she stopped grilling me, and I escaped to my room with my heart hammering like a prisoner on the wall of his cell. This time I got away with it somehow.

Good-night, Kitty

Translated from the Hebrew by Dalya Bilu

ESTY G. HAYIM was born in 1963 in Jaffa, and lives in Tel Aviv. She studied drama at Tel Aviv University as well as classical and modern dance. Hayim has worked as an actress, performing at the Cameri Theater and in plays for youth on Israel TV. She has also taught ballet and staged plays in Israel and the USA. At present, she teaches creative writing at college, leads writing workshops and lectures on literature. Hayim has published two novels and a book of short stories, some of which have been included in anthologies in Israel and abroad. In 1995, Hayim won the *Haaretz* short story prize; she was awarded the Prime Minister's Prize in 2002.

Something Good Will Happen Tomorrow

Tel Aviv, Yedioth Ahronoth, 2003. 317 pp.

Esty G. Hayim

Something Good Will Happen Tomorrow

W

An excerpt from the novel

hen I tried encouraging you to talk about books I knew you liked, you shrugged me off with your "Enough, Ima, I can't right now," and disappeared into your room. You left me no choice. As always, I waited for you to leave for school and went into your room, opening the door slowly, tiptoeing as if entering a forbidden kingdom, about to be caught at any moment. An unmade bed—all the millions of demands I made were in vain. At least make your bed. Is this a room? It's a garbage dump! On the shelf, your schoolbooks and reading books were all mixed up, a desk piled with papers, notebooks, pens and chocolate egg dolls for assembling, hippopotamuses and chicks and small cars. Of all the various candies, you love any kind of chocolate, especially Kinder eggs with a surprise inside. A tattered felt kangaroo from your baby days lay on the office chair facing the computer. Even though you're older now, you still fall asleep with it clasped in your arms. You meant to bring it with you on our vacation, but when you went to bed on the first night it wasn't there. Why didn't you bring the kangaroo? I asked, and you replied dismissively:

I forgot. We didn't mention its absence again. As usual, I rummaged in the papers strewn on the desk, looking for the notes you leave yourself. They were usually there, revealing a hint of you and open to prying eyes as if left on purpose so I'd read them. The first time I did this my hand trembled. I reproached myself, remembering how I'd caught my mother nosing through my old diaries, and except for "yes" and "no" I didn't speak to her for a month. Your room was a shambles, quiet. I looked around as if you were still there. My hand opened drawer after drawer of your desk, hesitancy slowly vanishing and the thought, He's my son, I'm allowed to know things to protect him, encouraging me to continue to the last drawer. You're allowed to do this just for once, I thought, salving my conscience that protested, Stop! Stop right there! Two days later, I stood again outside your closed room. I opened the door with one movement, like a little girl prying open her piggy bank. Just once more. On the table, as if expecting me, there was a note of yours: *Just once I want—I dream that I—*

In the mornings I waited for you to leave for school. If you were late, looking for a book that had disappeared at the last minute, I pushed you a little too eagerly, You're late, you know? And when the front door closed behind you, I was already opening the door to your room. The notes were on the desk, waiting to be read.

This time I couldn't find them, as if you'd hidden them, playing a little game of hide and seek with me. I found some old dog-eared tests, and a big red 100 on the first page—you almost never bothered to tell me the results of your school tests—empty notebooks, a packet of marbles and a few pirated software programs for computer games that Yoni brought you once, but it was impossible to install them on the old computer. Ashamed and angry, as if you'd broken some secret rule, I brushed off a few of the papers with the back of my hand, and when I bent down to pick them up I found some pages from a notebook with a description of your English teacher, defined as "Okay," and how she read to you after class and was surprised that a boy of your age, who didn't come from an English-speaking background, spoke the language so well. What a jerk, you'd written, you'd think my English was something, it's just that the others are stupid. There were a few lines about the shits that bully you—they call you "genius" as if it's an insult, "loony" and "homo" as if loonies and homos aren't people too; they call you "stinking Ashkenazi" as if your origins have a bad smell. You wished bitter vengeance on them, like falling from the seventieth floor headfirst, or sliding down a school handrail made of razor blades. I was frightened by the creative violence I discovered, then I reluctantly leafed on, to a poem you'd written about the last dream you want to have, when Death is watching from the window. Not a bad poem for your age—I'd gotten used to going into your room almost every day, reading the hastily ripped out pages like a spy. But even though I knew your thoughts, written on scraps of paper, I always felt they were an independent entity that belonged only to you, and you, my silent son, were still a mystery to me, a secret—

On the back of a sheet of squared paper filled with algebra exercises, I found something I was perhaps looking for. Elinoar is so cool, you wrote, her house is full of velvet couches and paintings on the walls, like a museum. She's probably got seventy cats, every time another one pops up and you can talk to her for hours. It's a pity my Ima isn't like that, she's never allowed me to bring even a cat's tail into the house. It's a pity Elinoar's not your Ima, I thought as I crumpled the paper in my hand and threw it into the basket, let's see how she'd cope with you all day, every day. What's so smart about being with you for a couple of hours once a week, or every two weeks. You've got that face you put on for strangers, the polite tone that only they get to hear. I get the closed face and the impatient voice. When you came home in the afternoon and asked what there was to eat, I said, Nothing. There's nothing. You want to eat, go to Elinoar and eat there. I know that when you get back hungry all the thought processes get jumbled in your head, but I couldn't stop. Hiding behind David Vogel's *Married Life* I remarked that Elinoar's food was probably tastier than mine, even though I knew I was talking crap. If you want, there are vegetables in the refrigerator, make yourself a salad. And then, tired and hungry under your heavy black backpack, you exploded—Salad? Me—salad? You know I hate vegetables! And I threw the book at you, and yelled, I won't look after you when you get sick from eating junk food! When you dropped a glass of water and it shattered on the floor, I called you head-case and screwup and your eyes became shiny and damp,—I wouldn't have chosen you, I'd have chosen her for my mother! I fled to the bedroom and wept, my face buried in the mattress like a baby whose favorite toy has been taken away and smashed against the wall. I begged forgiveness, although it was too late. Words spoken sink into the blood and it's hard to get them out. I got up and made you a cheeseburger, spreading lots of mayonnaise and ketchup on the roll the way you like it, but by then you didn't want to eat. I tried being like Elinoar, smiling, literary, a sorceress, I even bought a few velvet dresses and considered dyeing my hair black and putting it into hairpins so it would fall down my back like hers, but it didn't help. My hair still straggled around my neck. I decided to stop seeing her, hoping that you'd stop too, but I couldn't keep it up, I too wanted to drink in her power that helped me live. At our next meetings, there was a corrosive liquid that seared me inside, and when we sat in her kitchen or went to a café, I asked offhandedly, taking a careful sip of coffee that went down the wrong way, So what did you do with Uri that he looked so happy when he came home from you? And she shrugged, and said, We just talked.

⁂

What's a bird? A little nothing, a pile of feathers…

    She never agreed to a cat. Because of Abba's allergy. Every time I brought home an abandoned kitten she'd slam the door in my face. Not in my house, she'd say. On my ninth birthday, [Abba] came home early, put down his bloated black case and took my hand. Let's go buy you a present. She usually buys the presents. From him too. Small things other people give as surprises in birthday party bags: whistles, harmonicas, books. I looked at him. Will you buy me a pet, Abba? I asked him, I want a pet. I've got to have a pet. Maybe Sammy the Snail, she laughed. I already had a Sammy that I let go because I got fed up with him just sticking to the side of the jar. He looked more like a thing than an animal.

    We put the cage with the bird on a chair in my room. By the bed. It looked at us, a blue parakeet with frightened eyes. Its thin toes grasped the plastic swing with the strength of a refugee.

128

Ima was in shock when she saw the bird. I'm not going to take care of it, she declared, going straight into attack mode. Don't worry, Abba said. The boy's promised to take care of it. It's his. Yes, she said, but in the end it'll be me changing the water and feeding it and everything. At first I took real good care of it. I changed its water and birdseed, and every day I put new paper on the bottom of the cage but it quickly got covered with little greenish spots of shit. Abba would mumble "Good morning" to me and the bird, and go off to his presentations. Abba, thank you, I called after him one day. He turned his head and said, I bought you a pet so you'd learn to be a human being.

I tried to encourage the bird, it got frightened every time my huge hand invaded its cage. When I did manage to get it out it would run into a corner of the room, between the cupboard and the wall, and stand there looking up at the high ceiling with a stupid stare.

I felt sorry for it. A poor parakeet that was supposed to think it was human. Who knows what kind of hybrid it thought it was. But sometimes it perched on my finger, submissive, almost devoted, letting me stroke its short back feathers, listening quietly to the crap I whispered to it, all kinds of confessions of love, and Ima watching us from the doorway pretending to be indifferent.

I thought about it at school. It's weird how you get attached to a creature that doesn't talk and makes no effort to get you to love it.

Eventually it got used to us and agreed to come out of the cage on its own and put one foot and then another on my finger. I fixed a corner for it in the living room, with food and water, and it ran around on the floor, chirping among all kinds of little Kinder dolls and becoming quite naughty.

One day I got home early. The math lesson was canceled and everybody went to the ice cream parlor. I went home. I opened the door with my key. Ima was supposed to be at some event. I flew into the living room to see how the parakeet was. It was standing erect and grave on my mother's finger, its long thin toes twined around it like rings. It gave a little cheep, "Hey, anybody there?"

I just wanted to see if it would come to me, my mother apologized. I stroked her soft feathered tummy, and hop, she came to my finger. Then my mother went on griping and saying that she couldn't get the cooking done because a bird's like a baby, you've got to be there for it all the time. She tried to ignore it, she said, but the bird ran around under her feet, flew close to the floor, and sometimes it just stood there, so tiny, you could easily tread on it, its black eyes staring into the air, yearning for the Australian outback its ancestors came from. It breaks your heart to see it like that. That's why she'd always been against pets, you become a collaborator in castration, a crippled bird, once a month you clip its feathers so it won't escape, spray it for bugs, imprison it in a cage, or the house, in a corner of the living room. In her opinion it's cruel to keep animals for your amusement. An animal should live with animals, not people.

The parakeet was with us for six months and it did us only good. I don't know what we did for it. Whether it felt we loved it. [My parents] didn't shout at each other then, because at six in the evening the bird folded its head under its wing and went to sleep and they were afraid they'd wake it. Ima stopped thinking it was bad to keep a pet bird. She talked to it and made all kinds of affectionate cheeping sounds as if it was her lost daughter. One afternoon she was cleaning the house and squeezing out the floor cloth. The toilet door was open. The parakeet took off and made a few short flights from my finger to the living room couch and back. I don't know how it got into the toilet bowl and the water flushed down on it. Maybe it landed on the squeegee or the rail, and before anyone could see, it fell into the dirty water that my mother was pouring from the pail, and the toilet was flushed.

I was mad at her. Abba blamed both of us, and said the cage cost almost three hundred shekels. But still he looked sad when he put the cage into the loft. Afterwards we all calmed down. A stupid death for a stupid bird, going down the drain like a piece of dirty toilet paper. Just a bird and I...

Translated from the Hebrew by Anthony Berris

YITZHAK BEN-NER was born in Kfar Yehoshua, Israel, in 1937 and studied literature and drama at Tel Aviv University. Ben-Ner is a writer of screenplays and plays, a film critic and a journalist. He also edits and presents radio and TV programs. He began publishing stories as a young boy, and his first book for adults appeared in 1967. He has published nine novels, two collections of short stories and novellas, and four children's books. Several of his novels and stories have been adapted for the screen, TV and theater. Ben-Ner has been awarded the renowned Agnon-Jerusalem prize (1981), the Bernstein Prize and the Ramat Gan Municipal Literary Prize. His work has been published in translation in four languages.

City of Refuge

Tel Aviv, Am Oved, 2000. 409 pp.

Yitzhak Ben-Ner

City of Refuge

M*y* chicks from the kibbutz and my chicks from Acre hardly knew one another, as the saying goes. Zamiri, who as a child and a youth saw himself as Arab and was proud of it like his pompous father, flatly refused to visit me on the kibbutz when I went back there. And look at him now: more Jewish than a Jew, lying and winking like a money-changer in Lillienblum Street and flattering like a collaborator. No racism intended. In Ruta's world there never were Arabs and Jews. There were human beings and there were turds. Jew? Arab? What did these identities ever do to help Nitznatz or Shahaf? They're both under the ground now, reservist soldier and PLO fighter—and their mother had to fight like a tigress for their final right to a brothers' burial.

An excerpt from the novel

I brought Shahaf to the kibbutz once, in the long holidays. He was sixteen then and I introduced him to his brother Netz, who was about seven years older than him and lived in bachelor quarters and had a spare bed. I said to him, Meet your brother, Nitznatz. He's older than you. That doesn't mean he's smarter than you—but for the time being you listen to everything he says. Then what does Hafi, Shahaf, say to me—and still in Arabic? I want to go home. Nitznatz,

133

who was always a bit on the arrogant side, said to him, That's what you all want to do, isn't it—go home to Akko, Haifa, Jaffa. So what? And to me he said, at last we're getting to see something of the Arab strain of the family. And Shahaf puffed out his chest a bit, still not taking the haversack off his back, and said indignantly: I really am an Arab. Is that a problem? And Netz said to him, if I were you I wouldn't boast about it round here. And then the arguments started, over occupied land and who had a right to it and who didn't, and I said, don't you see how much you have in common? And Netz said, not that much really. There's only one thing we have in common and that's you, the one who produced us. This made me angry: What's this about? Are you afraid of this little Arab. He's your half-brother, dumbo. You haven't met in sixteen and a half years. And Netz replied, listen, I could have happily gone another sixteen and a half years, without knowing this half-thing even existed. And Shahaf was offended and said he wasn't going to stay in a place like this and listen to racist abuse from Jews. And Netz was annoyed by this and he said to Shahaf, Come here, *ya kleine Araber*, and I'll give you the biggest thrashing you've ever had in your life, and Shahaf told him he was an ugly example of the arrogant Jewish fascist. I said to the younger man, what's the matter with you? Are you afraid of this Jew? He hits you—you kick him back. And I added, this is good, this is how things settle down and the talking begins, so now I'm leaving you alone together. And Netz asked me, just a moment, how am I going to explain to everyone who he is, the little Ahmed who's latched on to me? I said to him, don't be such a mean bastard. The two of you are exactly like your no-good fathers. What's to explain? One way or another, the *paskudniak*s here, if you belted them on the head with a sledge-hammer, they'd still only understand what they want to understand.

The truth is, they argued all the time. Towel-head and PLO supporter versus Jew-boy Zionist. Hafi insisted on being called not Shahaf but Hafiz. It was tough on the boy, as his feelings of Arab identity were only reinforced by his encounter with the enclosed, and decidedly Jewish, kibbutz society—and on his big brother too, uneasy about this alien and hostile implant that their mother, damn her eyes, had foisted on him. Hrahrahrah. And yet, if anyone tried to attack Hafi—his big brother immediately leapt to his defense, and this was someone who took his fighting seriously.

So the full length of the holiday they were quarreling, arguing, trading punches—and eating from the same mess-tin and pissing in the same bucket. Brothers, in a word. In the end, praise be to Allah, I saw some reward for my efforts; an impossible friendship sprang up between them. Afterwards, they went their separate ways. Netz married and had children on the kibbutz and Hafi returned to Akko, and went from there to study in Moscow, something his Franji father arranged for him. Medicine. My son the doctor. Congratulations, Ruta.

And so the tribe of Ruta includes a professor of international renown and a criminal and a divorced daughter and a *mujik* kibbutznik, and there used to be a qualified chemist and a history teacher and a terrorist. And an autistic angel. And Mother Ruta, Mammama Rutatata, is also the bereaved parent of two soldiers who fell in the wars of Israel and Ishmael, and three children who died and one unhappy murderess. Ruta and her ten children. Hrahrahrah…

Listen, I'm reckoned a crazy old woman, a *majnuna*—"eccentric", as they call it these days—and I don't give a toss. But I can distinguish between different kinds of things. My eyes run around all the time, like radar arms revolving.

Well, we are naïve and foolish where our children are concerned. We want—not I, I never demanded from them anything I couldn't or wouldn't give them—we want their respect for us to be like that which we felt for our parents. But even their contempt for us is different from the contempt we felt for the previous generation. Their contempt, I see this around me all the time, is open and arrogant and crude. Well, I'm not talking about myself. In my case, the chicks were ashamed of their crazy mother who had caused them shame, and were afraid of her. And other youngsters, like the Ishmaelites, had a certain fear of mad people. So this was my advantage. Hrahrahrhah. I meet young people here and there, who could be my grandchildren. These contemptible creatures—especially the Tel Aviv ones, Tel Aviv being a special strain—with them everything's more subtle and richer. Many-sided reckoning. Everything comes with its opposite. Every association also includes its converse. For us, at their age, it was much easier, living simply according to simple rules. Loving what you love—and hating what you don't love…

[And then] there was a war. Another war. A war before the wars, or a war after the wars, or a war between wars. I don't know. Lebanon. They got Netz there, beside the Litani river, in an ambush. On the kibbutz they dug a grave for him, and they also paid their respects to Ruta the *akruta*, Ruta the smart-arse, the bereaved mother. And then, after the funeral, Zamir came to me and said: Ruta, *ya ummi*, now our Hafiz has gone too, in Lebanon. His car was hit by a missile, from an Israeli helicopter. He started wailing and hugging me, which I can't abide, and I'm standing there, the bereaved mother in work-trousers and boots, and everyone looking on. Now, said Zamiri, you're bereaved twice over. I said to him, are these more of your lies? And he put his hand on his heart and cried—nu, well, this was his brother and his hero, and he was so proud of him. It's the truth, Ruta, he said. He was killed there. But on the other side.

What other side? I said to him. There's no such thing as one side and another side.

There certainly is, he said.

I said, there aren't any sides. It's all the same side. There isn't one side that's right and another that isn't. Even those who get killed aren't in the right. Why did they go to their deaths, in the first place?

And he said, they didn't go, they were sent. They fooled them.

Exactly, I said. They fooled them on both sides. And why did they allow themselves to be fooled? In the end, all sides are in the middle. The ones who kill, the ones who are killed—and the ones like us, who are left behind. Nothing more to be said.

And then I went and changed the tombstone in the kibbutz cemetery to a double monument. There were howls of protest at this in the swamp, *ya-ba-ye*, and Peretz, the permanent secretary, came to me and said: You must agree with me, Ruta, that this time you've gone too far, you've crossed the line, in more ways than one. For all our liberal principles and commitment to peace, we can't bury an Arab terrorist in our kibbutz.

That got me seething. More ways than one? How many are there? What's to bury? I shouted at him. You know that what's left of Shahaf has been shoveled into some hole in Lebanon. It's only symbolic, Peretz. So his crazy mother, his *Jewish* mother, who doesn't believe in symbols, will have somewhere to remember him, once a year.

I don't believe Netz would agree to share a tombstone with the enemy, the idiot went on to say.

Enemy?.. Brother! Brother, *ya tawil*, I said. Go and explain to those *mujik*s, who are still stuck in the thought processes of the forties, that both Hafi and Netz were victims of this doctrine of force. Enemy. Ally. Terrorist or freedom-fighter. So I, with my frail body, hrahrahrah, defended the double tombstone. Literally, physically. Ruta the grave-guardian. I wouldn't let anyone touch it. And since then, Netz's pompous wife hasn't spoken to me, and her children don't even know they have a Grandma-Ruta in a hole somewhere. And the kibbutz? Until now, I'd got on reasonably well with the—what do they call it now?—the "community"—because every community needs a cock like me, to perch on the dunghill and shriek out what everyone's whispering between themselves. Every village needs its idiot. Hrahrahrah. But the business with the tombstone fouled it all up for me. And then, on the day of remembrance, I and my slain children were not even mentioned in the kibbutz memorial ceremonies. Excommunication, no less. Hrahrah.

And who turned up on the kibbutz, to attend the graveyard revelries, if not Moishe Dayan, the *schwantz*, the arch-turd with the eye-patch? Everyone, of course, was scurrying around him. And there was no way that Ruta, with her big mouth, could sit still. I made my way to the bottom of the cemetery-mound, where he was standing with all the arse-lickers, and I called out to him: Hey, Moishe! And when he looked round, surprised, I asked him, what, don't you remember me? Ruta? Ruta the mammoth, platoon B... the field units... Acre prison... The secretary, Peretz the prick, whispered something in his ear and pointed to his forehead. A gesture meaning, take no notice, she's a fruitcake.

But the man from Nahalal village asked me: Ruta? Ruta who? I shouted back, that doesn't matter. Anyway, you won't be hearing any compliments from me. I'm just a simple proletarian, and you've become Moishe the Great—but along the way you've forgotten where you came from and which way you're heading. What would the old pioneers have to say about your betrayal—veering from left to right?

The numbskulls standing around, alarmed by the embarrassment I was about to cause them, whispered to me, Ruta, for pity's sake! We're in the middle of a remembrance ceremony—but there's no stopping Bulldozerruta when she's all fired up. *Ya habibi*, I called to him from below, and please excuse the familiarity, if this is the state we promised to set up, I'm here to tell you it's all gone pearshaped. All these achievements of yours—exporting tomatoes and peace with the Egyptians—they don't make up for the oppression and the discrimination. You've turned the First of May into a cut-price fancy dress party! I yell at him, incensed, and he, the one-eyed pirate, smiles that twisted smile of his to himself. Yes, I continue. You and your government. The best of youth. The pampered ones, that is. All depending on what you bastards do—and what you do isn't what you say, and what you say isn't what you think. To this day there's still a transit-camp in Rosh Ha-ayin and hungry people under canvas. And what's with the occupation? You've turned us into a nation of conquest. And you, Abu Jilda the bandit, small-time writer and fighter, turning up in khaki at the five-star "Kasaba" restaurant and going on from there to your whores. Stealing antiquities and eating shishlik with the Arabs. And they all say of you: King David and Berl Katznelson combined. Writer and fighter. What hypocrisy. And what do they call you behind your back? A machine of darkness, squashing everyone who shows his head above the parapet. And then I put a hand over my eye and saluted with the other hand and said: General Moishe Dayan. "Hero of Israel" from the New Year greetings cards. But we know who you are. Jackal. Hyena from Nahahal, that they used to call "Mehalul" And there are others, gray as sackcloth, who fought, and sacrificed and still believe in mankind, in work, in principles. Who will salute them?

Translated from the Hebrew by Philip Simpson

From the Classics

LEA GOLDBERG (1911–1970) was born in Königsberg, East Prussia (now Kaliningrad, Russia), and spent much of her childhood in Russia and Lithuania. She started writing Hebrew verse as a schoolgirl in Kovno. After receiving a Ph.D in semitic languages from Bonn University in Germany, she immigrated to Eretz Israel in 1935. Goldberg was a renowned poet and a successful children's author, as well as a theater critic, translator and editor. She was a member of the Shlonsky group of modern poets and published much of her early work in literary journals associated with that group. In 1952, she established the Department of Comparative Literature at the Hebrew University of Jerusalem, and remained its chair until her death. Goldberg published nine books of poetry, two novels, three plays, six books of essays and non-fiction, and 20 books for children. Her collected works as well as selections of her poetry, prose, plays, essays, and 16 additional books for children were published posthumously. She was awarded many prizes, including the Israel Prize in 1970 (posthumously). Her work has been published abroad in eight languages.

There Comes the Light, 1946;

Repub. Tel Aviv, Sifriat Poalim, 1994.

Lea Goldberg

There Comes the Light

Docter Nikitin couldn't figure out what was wrong with
Nora. He came twice a day and articulated various conjectures, hesi-
tantly and warily, adding every time as an obligatory admonition:
"Not nice, young lady, not nice!"

An excerpt from the novel

But on the fourth day, the fever dropped, the headache passed,
and all that remained in Nora's body was a pleasant languor and a
subdued, warm indolence.

This languor kept her in bed for ten more days, and those days
were so quiet and nice. The happiest days of that autumn.

The morning hours were so wonderful. The mother went back
to work and Lisa was also busy in her office from morning on. Only
the light padding of Tikla's bare feet was heard in the apartment and
sometimes her monotonous song, bringing to Nora's room fragments
of rustic words about a white lily and mint in the garden.

Now and then, rain would knock on the bright window of her
room, but most days were clear. And in the morning, broad shim-
mering flecks of sun landed on the rug before her bed.

Twice during that time, Lucy Kurtz came by to ask how she
was between one class and another, pressed for time but not rushing.

Her weariness and pretty frowziness added a graceful note to those peaceful hours, and her few soft words didn't disturb Nora's rest.

Every single morning, Aaron would come and sit at Nora's bed for a long time and talk with her. And every single day, as soon as she opened her eyes in the morning, Nora waited for him to come and listened closely, but not anxiously, to the footsteps climbing the stairs, and she could always tell his steps from those of others.

After he left, she'd ask herself if she really loved him, and her answer was usually negative. It was nothing but the esteem of friendship, nothing but the charm of the encounter. But in the hours when she lay there from the morning on and waited constantly, not thinking about anything else, she knew, from that happy expectation, that she did love him, only him, despite the absurdity of that love, the fact that he was almost the same age as her father, and despite her unwillingness to love him.

In the evening, before she slept, she wanted to call up his face in her mind's eye; she'd see his blue tie, his gray coat, his shoulders, his hands, his hair and the silver threads in it, but not his face. Only sometimes, in a dream, it would come to her for a brief moment, as if teasing her, and then it suddenly changed and became intangible.

Once, at dawn, she dreamed she was standing in the Bergman house at the big pier glass at dusk, braiding her hair. Suddenly in the mirror she saw him approach her from behind, stand behind her and smile. She immediately turned her face to him, to see him, to see him and not his reflection, and behold—he was her father. When she woke up that morning, her eyes were wet.

Aaron did not talk to her now the way he'd talked with her in the woods. His statements were longer and freer, they weren't cutting, and his words didn't have the same slight mockery, always under the surface in the words of older people when they talk with the very young. He would tell her about himself, his wanderings and his life, sometimes he'd stray into abstractions, landscapes he had seen, books he had read. Maybe it was the peace of Nora's small room that imbued him with the grace of good conversation, and maybe he loved to see her listening to him talk, her absorbing eyes taking in his words. And Nora was a little proud that he always chose those

morning hours when she was alone in the house, and that he came
only to her, only for her.

Once, as he sat like that at her bed in a crumbled calm, smoking a cigarette, she said to him:

"I'll remember these days. I'll remember everything. The room,
the purple chrysanthemums on the table—Lotte brought me those
yesterday—and you in that armchair with lines of sun cutting the
smoke coming out of your mouth. After many years, I'll remember
all the details. Even if I'm very old. I almost always know in advance
what will stay in my memory. I'll even remember the sunspot on
your nose."

He moved a bit, rubbed his nose absent-mindedly as if he
wanted to wipe the sun off it, and Nora saw how the glowing spot
played on his long, tobacco-yellowed fingers. Then he got up, tapped
the cigarette ash into the white glass ashtray on the table, and said:

"Memories are the main thing, Nora."

And he sat back down in the armchair.

"Memories make us what we are. Precisely because we remember little things—unimportant things as it were, but so much ours.
When I remember my youth, for some reason I remember more
than anything else our bedroom, in my parents' house. On winter
nights. There were four long, narrow beds in it. My younger sister
slept on one of them and my two brothers on the other ones. And
my bed was made up, but I hadn't yet laid down in it. I used to read
standing up back then. And for some reason, the lamp in our room
was placed on a tall cabinet. Apparently so the light wouldn't be too
bright and disturb our sleep. The light stayed on all night because
my little sister was afraid of the dark and every now and then she'd
wake up at night. I'd stand between the stove and the cabinet, so a
very weak light fell on the pages of the book. I remember reading
the poems of 'The Painter,' my head ablaze with excitement. And in
the stove, some little door was always shaking, its iron was crum-
bling, and one shutter that was always broken would rattle and slam
outside. As if they left those things broken and didn't fix them on
purpose so we'd always remember them, so they'd always be part of
our life, our being."

He got up, put his cigarette out in the ashtray, then stood at the bookshelf and ran a fingernail along the volumes, as children or virtuosi run theirs over the piano keys. Then he pulled out a book of Verlaine's poems, bound in gray with a red leather back, opened it, read the title page, closed it and put it back on the shelf. Nora watched his movements, as if she were following some suspense drama.

He came back to her bed, stood there and said very slowly:

"I read the poems of 'The Painter.'" And stubbornly, he drew up from his memory:

> Still serenity all around,
> A strong wind will then awaken.
> On the cliff, the poet sits,
> Solitary, forsaken.

"What didn't we read back then into those verses! Understand me: not from them, but *into* them," he emphasized. "It's hard for me to imagine now, but I remember that's how it was."

He sat down.

"Did you write poetry in your youth?" he asked. And from that "in your youth," Nora sensed that he didn't see her at all at that moment.

"No," she said. "I never wrote poems in my life."

"I did," he said.

"I know. Spanish. Siempre Vago."

"Spanish," Aaron laughed. "And other languages, too. What they all had in common is that they were all bad."

And he laughed a little. A timorous smile hung on the ends of his lips.

"But memories," he continued. "They're what give us our private, individual tinge, they make us what we are. The facts of our life—with all that's wonderful in them at times despite everything—they're common property. We share them with others. And only what remains in our memory, even the most unimportant things, they're what constitute our real being. Let's say they're like the culture a person puts into wine. All the barrels are filled the same, you can't tell them apart, then along comes the head of the winery and puts the tiniest thing, let's say a culture of vermouth, into one of the barrels. That barrel isn't just wine anymore. It is all vermouth. It has its own special nature, a special essence."

"And bad memories constitute a bad nature?" Nora asked.

"There aren't any bad memories," Aaron said. "There is only a bad relation to memories."

"No," said Nora and her face became resolute. "There are bad memories. Definitely bad ones. I know it in the most objective way."

Aaron looked at her closely and said:

"Yes, I was wrong. There are very bad memories."

Nora blushed. She didn't like winning the argument, and so easily too. In fact, she really wanted him to prove the opposite.

But he said: "It's not a matter of good and bad. It's not a moral matter at all," and again he looked at her and added: "But once, remember, in the woods, you promised me something? And nevertheless you go on thinking about it."

"No," Nora apologized without asking what he meant. "I was thinking about something entirely different."

He didn't ask what, fearing that he might touch the most secret and painful wound. But she went on:

"You said: concerning the smallest and least important things. I thought of an unimportant case. But I'll never be able to forget it. It was this summer. At the end of June. It was one o'clock on a Saturday, very hot and stifling. All my friends were out of town. I had a month-end 'drought.' To put it simply: there wasn't a penny in my pocket so I stayed in the city. There was a heat wave. A stifling blaze. And I felt so lonely and abandoned in the big empty city. As if all my friends had died and I was left alone. Or maybe, to be more precise, as if they were all alive someplace else, and I had died and was walking around the streets and would always have to walk around like that, alone, in that awful heat. I don't know, but that's about how I felt. And after I ate lunch in a cheap, ugly restaurant, I was going home, thinking all those thoughts. And suddenly, around a corner, a fat man burst out at me, you know. With a beer belly and a ruddy, smug face. He looks me in the face brazenly, under my hat brim, and states with quiet confidence:

"Selbstmord."

She fell silent and her face grew angry, as if that man were still in front of her.

Aaron nodded:

"I imagine your face at that moment!" He smiled, but a minute later his eyes grew gloomy: "That is all very violent and very, very German. I wouldn't want to live in that country."

Nora leaned on her elbow and raised her head:

"It has nothing to do with Germany."

Aaron didn't answer that remark. She shrugged and said:

"And the main thing was, it was the truth. I was, in fact, close to suicide. What that man said was a kind of confirmation. As if he were the messenger of certain forces leading me in that direction."

"But you stayed alive!" said Aaron.

Nora bit her lip. And her face, which had turned pale as she was telling the story, blushed again, as usual, from the tip of her nose to her earlobes:

"I always stay alive, always!"

Aaron laughed aloud:

"That's good, Nora! Very good. Life is precious. Life is worth more than all our suffering. Only life."

He had a brief and strange attack of nervousness and started pacing the small room, measuring it with his big strides. Then he stood still, both his long hands leaning on the desk, and looked beyond it, out the window, to the courtyard.

"But remember this day, Nora. Remember it well, mainly what I just told you. I said that life is precious. In spite of everything. Because there's no catastrophe and no physical or mental illness that can lower its value. None. These things you have heard from me, Nora. It is I who said them."

From her bed, she saw only his ear and a thin crescent of his cheek. She didn't know if he was laughing or serious.

That day, after he left, she wanted to sum up what she thought of her life, and couldn't.

She put her hands under her head and lay supine, without thinking. In the dining room, the bell sounded two long full rings.

Now in her mind's eye, she saw Aaron's absent face clearly, including the fleck of sun on his nose. And once again she knew she would remember it like that forever. She was languorous and happy in her languor.

Translated from the Hebrew by Barbara Harshav

A Story

JUDITH ROTEM was born in Budapest, Hungary. She spent several months as a baby in Bergen-Belsen, and was then taken on the "Kastner train" to a refugee camp in Switzerland. After immigrating to Eretz Israel in 1945, she married an ultra-Orthodox yeshiva student and supported the family as a teacher, while raising her seven children. In 1983, she divorced her husband and left the ultra-Orthodox community, taking her children with her. She subsequently worked as writer and editor of hi-tech publications and published articles on various subjects in several newspapers. She has also ghost-written numerous autobiographies and books for Holocaust survivors. Rotem has published three novels, one work of non-fiction and a collection of stories. Her books have been translated into English, German, Italian and Hungarian. She has been awarded the Prime Minister's Prize (2002), and the Book Publishers' Association's Golden Book Prize for her bestseller *I Loved So Much* (2004).

A Footstool in Paradise

Tel Aviv, Yedioth Ahronoth, 2005. 186 pp.

Judith Rotem

Play Me the Appassionata

In our community you don't go out walking on Shabbat with less than five children. But I, with my three, do: defiantly, with dark rouge on my cheeks, bright lipstick on my lips, a black line on my lower eyelids and another carefully drawn narrow one above them.

Every Shabbat morning my husband waits for me in the street with the children. I peep from the window, seeing how he steals upward glances. His heart tells him that at this very moment his wife is transgressing the Law—"painting," one of the 39 proscribed acts of work on Shabbat. Punishment for the person who breaks this grave proscription is excommunication, God save us.

I take my time over my makeup. Go out into the street on Shabbat with dim eyes, faded lips and colorless cheeks? Out of the question. My face is my own. I'm also not prepared to give my friends and neighbors the satisfaction of pitying me. I don't want to be in their mouths, like Malki: "Poor thing," they tinge their voices with compassion, "the way she looks, simply awful, and how neglected she is. Ah, well, what she goes through…"

Malki, my sister-in-law Sari's sister-in-law, makes everyone she meets listen to her recount the treatments she's undergoing, the blessings she received from this great rabbi and that great Lithuanian Torah sage. She's not even shy of showing the amulet inscribed for her by the renowned Sephardi kabbalist. The neighbor, a Bratslav Hasid, brought her a small coral stone direct from Uman as a "remedy" and she fastens it to her bra strap with a safety pin. She points to it with her finger, out of modesty. "Don't ask how much it cost," Malki says excitedly, sharing a secret in her piping voice. "He didn't want to take any money, nor did his wife. Righteous Jews, I'm telling you, righteous Jews."

In exchange for her candor she expects me to tell her about my own problems. Am I crazy? Do I need her talking about me behind my back, Heaven forbid? So that all the women nod their heads and say: "God save her soul!"?

"Thank God," I reply dryly, "everything's fine with me."

Malki stays on with vague excuses as if to say, good, but where are we going with that thankgodeverything'sfine? I've told you my troubles, you tell me yours. Friends or not?

"I'm sorry, Malki, we'll talk another time, Miri's waiting for me at her friend's," I apologize and I'm up and away.

My problems are my own.

The women of our community are biblical—"And she conceived and bore, and she conceived and bore," and only Malki and I are not among them. My sister-in-law Sari, who's thirty like me, has had her tenth child, and Yochi, Zehava and Adina have got eight and nine. I stopped at three, to the shame of my husband who's concerned he'll be viewed as "modern," or even worse—"he obeys a woman." And what a woman, heaven forfend. One that insists on using "contraceptives."

Malki cares a lot about what people say. I don't. My womb's my own, isn't it? My husband's sure there's a connection between my stopped-up womb and the transgressions I never cease committing. Every Shabbat my rouge is brighter, the lipstick deeper and the line above my eyelids, like the one beneath them, becomes narrower and slants more. But my husband doesn't despair. Every Saturday evening he starts hoping that next Shabbat—God willing—the evil nature of vanity, coquetry and frivolousness will be excised, like a cataract.

And every Shabbat I break my promise. "You're making me a laughing stock!" say his eyes as I emerge from the yard. Dolled up as usual I walk down the alley steps, my high heels tapping, belt tight around my waist, and without a word I take my eldest son Moishi's hand. My husband's lips tighten into a line.

Every Shabbat, after the *Kiddush* and the cakes, our little family goes on a "visit." This is the Shabbat rule. We go to my sister-in-law Sari's or to one of my husband's friends. On the balconies of the stepped houses, all movement stops until we disappear from sight. I can feel every look shot at my slim figure, my long, curly chestnut wig, my lipstick-red lips, my provocative walk. Yochi, Adina and Zehava giggle self-righteously: "Just three children in two pregnancies! So it's hardly surprising she looks like that." Their husbands hush them: "Shhh... slander... slander..." They steal glances at me too. My bitterness is mixed with satisfaction. Let them talk. Let them look. May their eyes drop out.

My husband buries his eyes in the ground, and he holds tightly onto the hands of the ten-year-old twins Miri and Yuda. His knuckles whiten. When he perspires, his beard and hair become ruffled. He doesn't have a handkerchief with him and he wipes the sweat off with the back of his hand, wondering whether to reproach me, as it is written: "Reprove your friend lest he sin and you be guilty"—and a wife is a friend, at the very least—or whether he should restrain himself, for according to the Sages, "Just as it is wise to say something that may be heard, so it is wise not to say something that may not be accepted..." He'd very much like to tell me something, to threaten me with excommunication, which means my destruction in this world and the next.

But he decides to keep silent. I can hear the sound of swallowing in his gullet. Each wrapped in silence, alone.

On Shabbat the wide street in the center of town becomes a boardwalk. The women push before them their strollers and their bellies distended from the last birth or the expected one. The men, with hands as empty as their pockets, adorn themselves with the severity they impose on themselves in order not to rely on the *eruv* that encircles the community and limits movement. Small children clutch their fathers: "Abba, lift me up," and the fathers reproach them mildly: "Have you forgotten it's Shabbat today?"

Sometimes we meet Moishi's *rebbe* walking along with short Shabbat steps in his long Shabbat coat, surrounded by his wife and children. The *rebbe* comes up to my husband and talks to him quietly. We women move away, so as not to appear inquisitive and exchange a few words on women's matters. The *rebbe*'s wife scans my stomach surreptitiously, maybe something has changed since last Shabbat. The men talk, their heads bent. They are the same height. Their beards intertwine like two branches. The wide-brimmed hats swallow up their words. After a short while the *rebbe* bids my husband farewell with a half bow. He gives me a half glance and mutters: "*A gitte Shabbes.*" I ignore his wife, and say "Shabbat Shalom" in a sharp voice that conceals-and-reveals a hint of complaint and crumbs of disgust.

At the *heder* where Moishi and Yuda study, they use the Ashkenazi pronunciation. My husband didn't ask my opinion on this matter. The boys' education is his domain, no?

⁂

"You're like a couple of turtle doves, you never-ever-ever raise your voices," exult Yochi and Zehava and Adina. Even my neighbor Miriam praises us: "I can only hope that my daughters who, God willing, will stand under the wedding canopy one day, will have a family life like yours." To a certain extent my husband's righteousness cancels out my wayward characteristics. Everybody knows how he doesn't speak on Mondays and Thursdays and only prays, the nights of study he spends between Thursday and Friday morning, his insistence on observing the Sabbath laws. People wonder how a God-fearing Torah prodigy like him came to marry a worthless woman like me.

Ours was an arranged marriage. My well-to-do parents promised to support us as long as my husband studied the Torah. I was the second of four daughters, rebellious, problematic and defiant in my dark beauty, and my father married me off quickly before my bad name became known and spoiled my sisters' chances of marriage. My husband is tall and thin, a withdrawn ascetic. At our few meetings

156

before our engagement, I gazed into his face and hungrily devoured his every word. His talks with me were few and deliberate. His silence exuded strength, and I thought I would draw strength from him.

My groom exiled himself to Torah study until our marriage so as not to be diverted by the lust of the flesh. In his letters, written on long pages in his slightly cursive handwriting, he told me of his spiritual aspirations: that I be his helpmeet and build a home with him founded on the Torah and fear of God. In conclusion he added: "I shall be glad and rejoice in you." Sometimes he quoted the passage from the scriptures that testified to his repressed feelings, and he signed: "Your groom who awaits redemption."

A month after the wedding, tired from the "rejoicing of groom and bride" and my early pregnancy, I sat in front of the mirror in our room and readied my face for the night. Behind me, my husband was sitting on his bed and I was talking to him as a wife does to her husband. Perhaps I talked too much. While I was speaking, I looked for his face in the mirror but the mirror was empty. I went out of the room to look for him. He was standing at his lectern in the living room, swaying over his book.

To us talkers, people who don't speak much are seen as carefully guarding their secret and fascinating personality. We knock on their doors, throw ourselves at their feet and are pushed away.

When his silence thundered in my ears, I talked a lot. Before his blank face my every word reverberated like a shout in an empty cave. "Say something! Speak! You're hiding behind a dike and a moat and a wall!" I screamed inside myself. In the second year of our marriage his silence gripped my throat like a noose and almost destroyed me. Very slowly, I, too, sank into silence, either from dejection and despair, or in the hope that this way I would get him to like me. I wanted to show him that I could be silent too. As time passed, my words died like plants withering in the cold.

Silence is one of the only things that exist between us. My silence is both speech and scream. You just have to listen to it. What does his silence contain? I don't know. Perhaps the drawer I tried to break open with all my strength is empty after all?

If talking is a habit, all the more so silence. Perhaps he swore an oath not to speak to me. The muteness to which he sentenced himself began on one of those Mondays and Thursdays when he didn't speak. Perhaps he expected me to stop painting my lips and eyes on the Holy Sabbath when painting is forbidden.

Inside myself, I debated with him: Yom Kippur Eve, when vows are canceled, is still far off. So why do you stop me from speaking? Is this how you respect your wife, with your silence, when it is your duty to respect her more than your own body? Am I unworthy of the gift of your speech? Are you afraid that your speaking to me will defile your purity?

My husband came home from that parents' meeting red-faced and angry. His mouth opened as if he wanted to say something, and closed like the mouth of a fish. But in the matter of Moishi he could not remain silent. Torah study, not to mention that of schoolchildren, is something priceless, as important as honoring one's parents and giving charity, welcoming guests, going to funerals, making a match, and even—making peace between men, and between man and wife.

For a long time my husband thought about what to do. In the end he found a suitable substitute for speaking. On a sheet torn from a writing pad, he wrote and erased and wrote, and finally put it down under my blanket.

"The *rebbe* has complained, and he hinted about it last Shabbat: Moishi dreams in the lessons, and when he is not daydreaming, he is disruptive. He asked if perhaps there is a problem at home, and suggested that his wife talk to you, from the aspect of: 'If a person has worries, let him talk them over,' or in other words, 'talk them over with someone else.' His wife has great experience in matters of domestic harmony. People come to consult her, to pour out their troubles. Please call her."

Signs of life in the wilderness, I said to myself. The cat's out of the bag and the tongue of the mute is unfettered.

Over the next few days the notes kept on coming, at first in a trickle, then in a torrent:

"I spoke to the head of the *kollel,* the religious college, Rabbi Arieh Friedman. I told him. He wants to speak to you. To help. I would very much like you to, if not out of respect for me then out of respect for Rabbi Friedman. And for the children's sake…"

"My mother plans to come tomorrow, God willing. She hasn't seen the children for a long time. You don't have to prepare anything, she will bring all the food with her and she will be at Sari's for Shabbat. I hope you'll know how to behave. You know she's not in the best of health. Try not to cause her sorrow. Honoring one's mother…"

"Sari asks that you call her. Why don't you ever return her calls? You're sisters-in-law, aren't you? And why, when she finally gets hold of you, are you so impatient? After all she's done for you…"

I tear the notes into tiny shreds and spread them over his blanket. As far as I'm concerned, he make a mosaic with them. You've gone too far with this game, I think, claiming my right to silence with an unfamiliar passion.

It seemed that the small house had shrunk and could no longer contain both of us. Our silences swelled around us like huge unperforated featherbeds. My husband was angry and his eyes avoided me and the children. Only when the neighbors come in—the doors in our community are always open—he welcomes them and a rare smile unlocks his face, spreading the tiny lines at the corners of his eyes into a fan and softening the stern lines that start by his nose and end only in his beard. In those moments, I wonder how not even one of my sharp-eyed, sharp-nosed women neighbors has detected anything. Even the children take part in the game, as if it were real life. With good spirits they act as go-betweens—or so it seems—"Tell Ima," "Give Abba," "Ask Ima," "Tell Abba." The children, I ask myself, whose are they, mine or his?

The days and months pass, who can count them? Our silence thickens. If it had any grounds at all, the passing time has dulled and diminished them.

Until something happened to awaken a memory in me that I promised myself I would forget—muted notes, a piano whose playing was silenced.

A new family moved into the house across the street. Yochi,

who always knows everything before anyone else, told me that the mother had died and left five children. Her face had an appropriately sad expression, but it was immediately replaced by its usual effervescence. Her short eyelashes flickered with excitement, her speech was rapid: before he "repented," our new neighbor had been a famous singer and musician, admired all over the country. He was engaged in music now too, not secular—godforbidheavenforfend—but "our" music. His rabbi had given him a special dispensation, and he'd also changed his name from Nimrod, the name of that king of whom it is said: "He knows his sovereign and intends to rebel against him." Now he's Hezkiahu, which means "he who finds his strength in God."

Yochi looked at us anxiously, waiting for our amazement at the news, but instead Sari and Malki bombarded her with questions: how old are the children? When did his wife pass away? Can we suggest a match to him? And Adina, the most suspicious of all, asked: "How do you know all this?" Yochi was hurt and replied reproachfully: "What do you want of me? I know, and that's it! What do you think, that I've got a television set in the bedroom like some people here? All I've got is a broken down radio that I barely get to listen to when everybody's asleep and I'm ironing, before I fall off my feet."

Adina got up to leave in protest at the implied criticism, and Yochi leapt up, begging her to stay: "Oh, really, I didn't mean anyone in particular. If I've hurt you, I ask your forgiveness…"

Next day I didn't leave the kitchen window. A huge truck with green tarp sides was unloading its contents. My heart pounded wildly at the sight: three guitars, a trumpet, a xylophone, a saxophone, two clarinets and two drum kits. Did he intend to start an orchestra here? Not a bad idea, I said to myself, and my heartbeat returned to normal.

It seemed that the truck was revving up, as if about to drive off, when I heard an unfamiliar voice. "Hey, guys, watch the piano. I don't want even the tiniest scratch. It was my wife's, her most treasured possession."

The two brawny porters were now standing at the edge of the truck bed. Another was standing below, legs apart, ready to receive the cumbersome instrument—black, polished and with carved lion's head legs.

It hasn't been with us for a long time, that piano we called "Shuli's Beckenstein." I sent it to my sister Rivki, even though Miri cried so much. I just couldn't see it in front of me all day every day. Reminding me of a sin. His, mine, ours?

More than Shuli's, my younger sister, it was the fulfillment of my mother's dream. She had found her way to Israel after the war without parents or family, and all she wanted in life was to give her girls a musical education like the one her parents had given her in Pressburg-Bratislava. But only Shuli was lucky enough to get it, after my father gave in to my mother's pleading and finally allowed her to accept the reparation money from Germany that she was entitled to. "You can buy what you want with your tainted money!" he shot at her, and she bought a piano, like the one she had "at home."

After my mother fell ill and passed away, I longed for the splendid black piano with its carved lion's head legs and regal appearance. I maneuvered so I'd get it. Shuli, my younger sister, was about to get married to the son of a family of Antwerp diamond merchants, and before Rivki the eldest and Miri the musical one managed to discuss it, my father saw fit to give it to Miri, his beloved granddaughter.

Back then we lived in a rented house in the old part of the Baron's *moshava*. The painted floor tiles resembled terracotta carpets with turquoise and gold, the big windows were decorated with colorful stained glass and the heavy, three-part wooden doors were ornamented with bas-reliefs carved by an artist. An avenue of palms led to the front door and a splendid entrance supported by sculpted portico columns, like a Greek temple.

I was saddened by the house's emptiness. My husband, the founder of the local *kollel*, subscribed to the Lithuanian Novharduk yeshiva school of thought, which practiced modesty and abstinence. A home is for living in, not self-adornment, he claimed. Furniture must be functional. Beds, tables, chairs and cupboards must be the essence of simplicity. Any deviation from this principle is nothing but luxury, and luxury—as its very name tells us—is unessential, too much of a good thing. My husband even refused to accept a phonograph in the house. With my own money I bought a few records—Grieg's *Peer Gynt*, Dvorak's *From the New World* and Beethoven's piano sonata in F minor, the *Appassionata*, and one evening every week I'd listen to my records at Malki's, on a scratchy phonograph her husband had inherited from his parents. I loved the *Appassionata* most of all, its notes cascading one after another, striking one another, tormented, expressing love, passion, doubt, pain, and finally, purification.

As much as I tried, I was unable to overcome my vain desires. The piano hadn't yet been brought to my house and I was already imagining it against the northern, main wall of the living room, covered with crocheted cloths and decorated with art objects I'd bought with love, and my own petit point embroidery in polished gold frames. That imaginary scene was so beautiful, so alive and pleasurable that I felt, without knowing why, that I'd do better to erase it.

And I immediately told myself, didn't the Sages say that the home is the wife's kingdom, for a man's wife is his home and all his possessions, and she is a princess in it?

A week before Shuli followed her husband, the piano was brought to our house. Unexpectedly, my husband came home in the afternoon. The sweating porters loaded the huge instrument onto their backs—it was like an elephant that had been given a huge anesthetic—and carried it up the steps to the entrance. I opened the folding door wide and told them where to put it, but my husband cut me off with a gesture. "Over there!" he ordered, and in a flash the porters turned around and carried the piano in the direction his finger indicated.

It was taken to the back of the house, the utility room that served as a storeroom and study and playroom. After the porters left and my husband returned to the *kollel*, I walked over to it slowly. The piano stood among suitcases and children's bikes and an ironing board and a wicker basket full of laundry waiting to be folded, and cans of olives and pickled cucumbers and a cupboard containing the Passover dishes, and all the other things a family needs but does not want in view.

From close up the piano seemed like a lion in captivity. I slowly pushed it away from the wall, first moving the basket and cans of pickles. I went around the washing machine and sewing machine, bent under the clotheslines strung ready for winter, squeezed through the doorway, continued into the big hall and from there, through the passageway, I finally reached the living room. I was perspiring a little and didn't know if it was from the physical effort or the excitement. Sharp pains pierced my lower stomach, but I continued, sweating more profusely now, until I'd pushed the sublime object into its designated place.

I don't know if it took minutes or hours. In my mind I could hear Miri playing Chopin waltzes and mazurkas, Bach fugues, and Beethoven's *Moonlight Sonata*. My fingers, which had never played the piano, were tingling with desire. I saw my beautiful daughter playing at a student recital at our neighbor's, Lily Samuelov, the piano teacher who had nurtured generations of pianists. Miri was wearing a white lace dress and a blue velvet ribbon in her hair, and the teacher stroked her fair hair and said: "Your daughter played the best of all. She has a brilliant future, but with you people it's no simple matter, is it?" And I replied: "Why? My daughter's future is in my hands."

Filled with power I went back to the utility room and set up the ironing board. There were piles of white shirts waiting for me. My husband changes his shirt every day. Each day and its pristine shirt, for a Torah scholar with a blemish on his clothing puts himself at risk. Afterwards I fed the children and put them to bed. The stabbing in my stomach turned into a dull ache that slowly became sharper, then turned inward as if towards the center of a whirlpool, pinched like black sand crabs, and broke in waves inside me. When my husband came home late, I lay down to rest on Miri's bed, hugging her to my swelling body.

Towards morning Miri woke me with her crying: "Ima, it wasn't me! Ima, I promise you, I don't know who did it!" The frightened Moishi and Yuda looked at me wide-eyed from their beds. My husband was standing by the bed without a yarmulke, in his pajamas and yellowing, woolen, ritual tassels, as if he'd just jumped out of bed. I was cold. I was wet and sticky and my clothes were crumpled.

Miri and I were lying in a pool of blood. I gripped her hand, pushed her to the edge of the bed and didn't dare get up.

I suddenly had a flash of an interrupted dream: I was on my way to school with Rivki, Hanni and little Shuli whose face was Miri's. The school, which was at the bottom of a hill, stood like an island in the center of a dark puddle. Rivki and Hanni, and even little Shuli-Miri, had already slid into it and come out unsullied on the other side; only I stood hesitating and they were laughing at me: "Come on, you scaredy-cat, slide already!" Then I took my schoolbag from inside my stomach, an aching void opened up in the middle of my body, but I ignored it, sat on the bag and slid down into the thickmurkyredwater…

At the hospital the doctors examined me, competing with one another with their grave expressions: What did you do? Your sixth month? Have you a history of miscarriages? Was your husband home? Did you get a bang? An accident? Did you fall?

I wept soundlessly. The head of the department stroked my head: "I'm sorry. You're going to lose the baby. We've got to deliver it quickly and clean up properly inside, otherwise there'll be complications. Why are you crying? You've got three healthy children at home. Do you know how many women would willingly change places with you?"

When I came round from the anesthetic my husband was sitting on a chair, his eyes in a book. He was looking away and distancing himself from me, so he wouldn't have to touch me, the bleeding, unclean, sinful woman.

"It was a boy," he said flatly, turning the book over and over. "It is obviously a punishment and you know exactly what for. The Almighty, Blessed be He, yearns for the prayers of barren women, but you're not barren. You were given, and it was taken from you." He opened the book and focused on its lines. "I'm not saying that I'm a paragon of virtue, I too have to examine my actions. At midnight prayer I shall examine myself thoroughly. Perhaps I have sinned by neglecting my Torah study, or prayed with insufficient devotion, or perhaps I sinned by speaking on Monday and Thursday."

I kept silent. He got up, slammed the book shut, but even at the door he avoided looking at me. His face was aflame, his hair and beard thinning into tiny curls. "It's late, I must put the children to bed"—and he left without saying goodbye.

Since then my womb has closed up. One miscarriage then another, and another premature birth after which the doctor scolded me: "Tell me, haven't you had enough? Do you want to leave your children motherless? What's with this obsessive race? Get yourself out of the competition!" I wanted to say to him: Gynecologist, what do you know about women? And what do you know about women like me? A doctor is given the power to heal, but how can he heal when my illness does not appear in the book of ailments?

My husband's mouth has been clamped shut since then and so has mine. Our hearts were locked so that the pain could not come out. The gate of tears, so near the gate of words, was closed. The tears fossilized and became stalactites and stalagmites in the caves of my heart. Perhaps someday I'll forgive him for the pain, but I'll never forgive him for turning me to stone.

Towards the evening when I had to go and purify myself, the notes on my bed went forth and multiplied. In silence I go to the ritual bathhouse, and the attendant, my friend Adina, removes the threads of long hairs from me and examines my lips to make sure that all the lipstick has been removed and that none remains between the cracks. The women waiting their turn see me when I arrive and leave, my provocative clothing and my makeup as garish as war paint—So does she use contraceptives or doesn't she? And perhaps we've just been gossiping about her? Their conscience starts pricking them, and at that moment they start counting, so if I get pregnant they'll know my date.

Instead of slamming the iron door of the *mikveh*, I close it gently behind me with demonstrative slowness. Enough already, my life's my own, a tiny voice screamed inside me, while another challenged: Go ahead, talk, talk about me, and be damned!

Silently I went into the empty room, removing my head covering, shaking out my damp hair. The beds had been moved together. The notes on my bed stared at me, waiting for me to read them. I spread the towel out to dry, put my toilet articles back in their place and sat down to read. "Malki is with child! The gates of mercy are not locked! And the gates of repentance are not locked either. We shall be with child if there is an opening as small as the eye of a needle!"

"Malki's husband gave me the name of a doctor, a rising star! I heard that he really admires learned Jews, perhaps you'll make an appointment to see him?"

And a damp note, like a mute carp pulled from a pond: "How long are you going to be so cruel to me?"

The early summer evenings are soft, still merciful. I sit down on the porch swing. A big mulberry tree stands between my house and the one opposite, and I can hear the sounds of the piano from there. Sometimes it's his confident playing that chokes the longing for the new neighbor, at others it's the dreamy, fluttering playing of his oldest daughter.

His children mix with mine. He comes to collect them in the evening. Their names are foreign to our ears here: Keren, Lilach, Tomer, Tom and Noga, all modern Israeli names. His appearance is foreign too. He's tall and thin, his brown hair longer than is customary and his beard shorter. He wears long dark shirts outside his pants and his fringed tassels hang below them. I follow him through the kitchen window as he hangs out washing or waters the lawn. When he goes to the shopping center I take off my apron, quickly get ready and follow him. I take Miri with me, who has no suspicions about my sudden initiative. At the supermarket, by the dairy refrigerator or the bakery shelves we nod a greeting. Noga, his little girl sitting in the trolley, is happy to see us. "Abba, can I come home with Miri's mommy?" and she twines her tiny fingers into mine. Her eyes grow large as she pleads. His eyes narrow as if he's having a fleeting thought. He agrees.

Sometimes he borrows two eggs or half a loaf, leaving my door open and hurrying back home. I sit at the kitchen table with trembling knees and melting heart. He doesn't send his children over to me like Miriam and Yochi. The presumption is so subtle... I relish the possibilities enfolded in it.

One evening I went over to his house. Close up he looked even taller and more tired. At the door I unloaded my request, as if ridding myself of a dangerous burden: if he's free, perhaps he would teach my son Moishi to play the drums?

"… the boy's bar mitzvah is next year but not one of his *rebbes* knows how to deal with him," I say in a begging voice, "he's alternately dreamy and wild and he doesn't have the slightest interest in his studies. I thought perhaps playing an instrument would help, the drums, so he'd use some of that energy. Perhaps you could…?"

Frightened by myself I let the words die, my eyes roaming inside the house, seeing everything: the spick-and-span kitchen that looked as if five children hadn't eaten in it, the colorful wool rug in the living room, light wicker furniture, the piano, and on it a portrait of a woman. Something in her smile troubled and attracted me at the same time.

"What does your husband say?" he answered me with a question and closed the door behind him. "Noga's asleep," he said apologetically.

We were standing on the front porch under a brilliant sky. You could almost hear the countless stars above us. They crackled quietly and delicately like those bubbles in plastic packaging, the ones that children like to pop between finger and thumb.

Suddenly, I solved the enigma of the face in the photograph. Filled with an unexplained happiness I slowly studied his face. "To tell you the truth," I replied, my voice ringing, "I haven't asked him yet. The children are my sphere, wouldn't you say?"

A damp note: "The new neighbor has agreed to teach Moishi the drums. I'm very surprised you didn't see fit to inform me. I'm warning you: you're on a slippery slope with no way out!"

I borrow his note system and leave sealed notes between the rocks in the next yard, inside the guitar case that's sometimes left on the patio, or inside a paper bag with a loaf he sometimes borrows. To be on the safe side I add warnings: "For H's eyes only! You have been warned! Anyone opening this envelope is violating a rabbinical ban!" My tiny, dense letters, asking to be decoded.

"Play me the *Appassionata*," I ask at the end of each note.

In my bed at night I imagine us in various forms, in distant places, in ways I'd never been with a man. My husband lies beside me, his face to the wall. I invent dialogues for me and my love. I speak and he replies, he speaks and I reply. My legs tremble. In my mind I wear the smile of the woman in the photograph. No one has ever seen an expression like that on my face, I know. I dream of myself beautiful and happy.

On the swing in the yard, visions grow in my mind like buds on the mulberry tree; they play like melodies floating to me from his fingers on the piano. I see myself in a white dress, barefoot, dancing in the middle of the lawn with him facing me. We're both little children. I sing, "Put your hand in mine, I am yours and you are mine," and each moment my voice becomes stronger, and we grow and grow to our present size. Our children are like olive saplings around us.

Evening falls. His children and mine are playing in the yard. From the house opposite, the notes on the piano are carried to me. I'm in the kitchen, using a small, sharp knife to slice meat for tomorrow's lunch, chopping vegetables for a meticulous salad, cutting bread into equal slices for supper. Slicing. Chopping. Cutting. Slicingchoppingcutting. The cutter cuts cuttingly. The chopfallen chopper chops chillingly, threateningly, and the slicer spreads her wings. Where to?

It is him playing. The tortured, yearning, pure notes of the *Appassionata* are carried to me from his house like messengers bearing a gift. His playing flows from his fingers to mine, into my ears and heart, filling my veins and arteries down to the tips of my toes.

Moishi waves to me on the way to his drum lesson. Soon I'll hear the echoing drums—those my son plays: still hesitant, lacking assurance but full of fervor, and those of my mystery man: strong, assured, sending me messages I must decode.

My husband comes into the house without looking at me. "Ask Abba if he wants to eat," I ask Yuda. My husband raises a hand like a wedge between us and goes into the bathroom. The children and I listen: faint sounds, dragging feet, water flowing in a heavy beat that stops all at once, and silence. The tumult of the house is absorbed into the walls and does not reach him. He doesn't answer when Miri, the apple of his eye, begs him to come out.

Why is he shutting himself in the bathroom? I peek at him through the keyhole. I've never seen him naked, just as he has never seen me unclothed. He's laying in the water, his beard in the air, his hands resting on the folds of his stomach under the water and his eyes are closed. The sounds of drumming come through the walls, loud, assured, intensifying all the time. My heart drums in response: Put your hand into mine, I am yours and you are mine.

My hand clenches inside my robe, recoiling from its contact with the cold knife blade. The door opens at my touch and I go in silently. The water is thickmurkyred…

Translated from the Hebrew by Anthony Berris

Interview

AMOS OZ was born in Jerusalem in 1939 and went to live at Kibbutz Hulda at the age of 15 where he worked in agriculture. Oz studied philosophy and literature at the Hebrew University of Jerusalem. For 25 years, he divided his time between writing and teaching in the kibbutz high school. In 1986, he left the kibbutz; he now lives in the desert town of Arad and teaches literature at Ben Gurion University. Oz has been a Visiting Fellow at Oxford University, Old Dominion Fellow at Princeton University, and author-in-residence at the Hebrew University of Jerusalem. Tel Aviv University and Colorado College, among others. Oz has published 11 novels, three books of short stories, seven books of essays, and a children's book. He has also published numerous articles and essays about the Israeli-Arab conflict, and is one of the leading figures in the Peace Now movement. In 1991 he was elected a full member of the Academy of the Hebrew Language. Oz has received many honors and awards. In 1984, he received the Officier des Arts et Lettres in France; in 1997, President Jacques Chirac gave him the Légion d'Honneur. He has also received the Bialik Prize (1986), the French Prix Femina Étranger (1988), the Frankfurt Peace Prize (1992), the Israel Prize for Literature (1998) and most recently, the Goethe Prize for literature (2005). Amos Oz's work has been published in some thirty languages in thirty-five countries.

Gershon Shaked interviews

Amos Oz

G.S.: I've recently read several autobiographies, including yours, and it seems to me that many of them deal with previous generations—that of parents and grandparents. In your novel, A Tale of Love and Darkness, *you hardly mention people of your own generation that you met at school or at university. Why are they missing from your novel?*

Oz: I'm not entirely convinced that I've written an autobiography or a memoir. I am not the protagonist of this book. My parents are the protagonists. My book covers their entire lifetime, essentially my life for the first fifteen years. Apart from one or two exceptions—my marriage, one day in Arad—it's not about my life, it's about them. I'm a supporting character, not the main protagonist, which is why I never describe it as an autobiography. You do, I don't.

It is true that I was a very lonely boy, not only because I had no brothers and sisters, but also because most of my childhood attention was diverted to the world of adults. Other children play games—cowboys and war games; I read newspapers. And I read the maps of the world and moved the pins on it. I was five. When I arrived in [Kibbutz] Hulda, rebelling exactly against this, they nicknamed me "the old little boy." I read the same in Amalia [Kahana Carmon]'s story about the old child and I thought she was talking about me. I came to Hulda, thinking I was going to change this and create a different self. I wanted to be born again, to be re-incarnated. I wanted to get suntanned, to be a simple uncomplicated tractor-driver. No more books, no more footnotes. My parents were short, I decided I would become very tall. It didn't quite work. But not even in Hulda did I manage to break my essential loneliness. This changed later in life. I'm not a lonely man now, I have friends. Not millions, but I have friends, but that is not part of this book. If I ever write *Love and Darkness Rides Again,* or *The Son of Love and Darkness*, I will talk about how I started to make friends after I married. And if this coincides with other autobiographical stories, or plays or memoirs or novels, fine. In there, you will find to some extent the lonesome Jew, from Joseph the dreamer in the Bible to Agnon's Hirshel and Yitzhak Kummer [in *A Simple Story* and *Yesteryear*] who had not one friend, so you'll find this type of lonesome dreamer very widespread in Hebrew literature.

G.S.: You write anecdotes in your novel about famous intellectuals and politicians such as Klausner [historian, literary scholar], Bergman [philosopher] and Menachem Begin. Your attitude towards Begin is quite sarcastic, but you speak of Ben Gurion with humor that has a great deal of love in it. So much love that I was surprised.

Oz: Both you and I, Gershon, we both said good-bye to our parents at a late stage in our lives [metaphorically, through our books]. Now, parting from one's parents does not just mean from mother and father. They had many reflections, and obviously Ben Gurion was a father figure to many of us. When you were in your twenties and I was in my teens, every single one of us—whether we were for him or against him, in his [political] party or in the opposition—saw him as an overwhelming father figure. And almost every one of us took part in the tribal ritual of slaying the father—I was one of the sharper knives against him. I wrote some things about him which obviously had very little to do with him, and more to do with my father and me.

But Ben Gurion was the father of the nation. And the tone in which I write about him is—you may notice—not unlike the tone in which I write about my own father, in spite of the huge differences between them. Ben Gurion was a great man, my father was not a great man, to say the least. Ben Gurion had gigantic dimensions to him, there was nothing gigantic about my father, except in the eyes of the little boy. Every father is a giant in the eyes of a little boy. But as I look at them now, Begin was different. Begin was a ridiculous, pompous uncle. Yes, I mean uncle. He reflects one or two family characters in the novel to whom I do not relate as warmly as I do to others. Even when I write about Bergman, or Agnon, or Tchernichovsky [the poet], it's still within the family. Now, have I covered the whole family? Of course not. There are people who have had some significance in my life and who are not in this book. You are not there, Dov Sadan is not there. I could mention half a dozen others, no, more, who were parents. You kindly called [my book] a novel just before. Yes, I did have some artistic considerations. There are certain things I would have done if I'd written a memoir, but that I knew I would not write in a novel. I will tell you a secret. There are probably 900 pages of manuscript which were edited out of the original text, because composing the novel was my hardest undertaking. Not self-exposure, not confession, but composition and structure. And for reasons of composition, I left out many members of the family.

G.S: The family as synecdoche of society—your novel offers a positive construction of the Zionist narrative. I think it's the most positive novel about Jewish Israelis in the last decade. It is written with an inquiring eye that does not ignore the weaknesses of Israeli society. It sees both the effort and the pain. But to talk about specifics, there seems to be no balance between the Klausners and the Musmans [Oz's two sets of grandparents] in your novel. The only Musman whom you fully characterize is Sonia, the aunt. But Grandfather Musman from Kiryat Motzkin, who is to my mind a pioneer, a man who came from wealth and became a cart-driver, he fades out of the novel. Why?

Oz: I wrote a lot about my generation in *A Perfect Peace*, in *Fima* and in a couple of other books. This book is about endless secrets, my beginnings before my beginnings. It is true that my Haifa grandfather fades away from the pages of the book like thin air as soon as Aunt Sonia finishes her story, and that's only a short episode. After that he is no longer there. For a prosaic reason: he lived in Kiryat Motzkin, he spoke only Yiddish, he never ever learned Hebrew. He was a cart-driver in Haifa—till the mid-50s one could manage in Haifa with Yiddish, also in Tel Aviv and Jerusalem. Not in the university but in the country. He lived his life in Yiddish, so sometimes he would talk to me and I couldn't understand, because my father was against my knowing Yiddish. But I think my own kind of personal rebellion, my own little "October revolution"—going to the kibbutz—is not unrelated to the story of my grandfather. And here I make a connection which I want you to think about: the movement from the Klausners to the Musmans. Becoming a tractor-driver was a strong slap in the face to the Klausners [as though I were saying]: since my grandfather was a cart-driver, I'm going to be a tractor-driver. He was a socialist, nearly a communist. I would be the same. And although my mother never told me—she wasn't allowed to tell me—she was [a member of] Hashomer Hatzair [socialist Zionist youth movement] as a young woman. At this point, I end the section [of the book]—so this is not an entire disappearance. They are still there, all the way.

G.S.: Amos, you've just given a very interesting interpretation of the novel. There is no connection in the text [between your move to the kibbutz and your grandfather's life-story]. But there is no reason why you couldn't have made this clearer. You've left gaps… Now I see the composition problems you had: you built a mountain and then wanted to create a tunnel through it. The first time one reads it, one doesn't notice all the stitches. I personally see a great effort on your part because you want to defend the Zionist narrative. On the other hand, there is also a rebellion against your own generation here.

Oz: Including against certain things I did forty years ago.

G.S.: Today, the left—to which you belong—is supposedly post Zionist, postmodernist. But people could argue that you don't have enough Mizrahi characters in your novel.

Oz: During my teens and my years at the kibbutz, I was part of the attempt to slaughter the old sacred cows. The way I wrote about the kibbutz was often seen by the old guard as very radical and subversive, and I was accused of being a traitor to the kibbutz. Some of what I have written about Arabs and Israelis or about the Arab-Israeli conflict was also regarded as subversive and uneasy. In recent years, as I watch the orgy of fifty slaughterers crowding around one dying cow, I begin to feel on the side of the cow. Not because the cow smells wonderful—it doesn't smell any better than it smelled to me fifty years ago—but because the cow is only one, and very ill, while the slaughterers are young, powerful and many. So many that they are a mob, a lynch mob. I will never be part of a lynch mob. I may have been very critical of the Zionist narrative, the kibbutz movement, and the labor movement, as long as this was an individual, and to some extent unpopular stand. The moment it became the best show in town, everybody started slaughtering the same cow, again and again. I really have a certain empathy for that cow. Besides, this is a cow that gave us milk. It may stink, it may smell bad, it may be an old cow and it may not have been a beautiful cow right from the beginning but that's where the milk came from. The slaughterers have yet not produced any milk.

Now I'm going to tell you something even more serious. This book has its face turned towards my ancestors: my parents, my grandparents, my mother, my father, Ben Gurion, Agnon, Tchernichovsky, but it is addressed to my children and grandchildren. They are the recipients. I was writing about the elders but I was writing about them for the sake of my children and my grandchildren, hence the need to explain things that I would not have explained if I had written this book for readers of the older generation. There would have been less historical chronology, for example, were I writing for people in their seventies and eighties. No, the addressees are my children and hopefully one day my grandchildren, because I had to apologize to them, I had to defend myself. They find themselves in a situation which is not rosy, not wonderful. They have every right to come to me and say: that's not what you promised us, that's not what parents owe to their children.

Now to the other thing. There is a radical process—universal and not just Israeli—of quick erosion of the hard disc of collective memory, that is quicker and more destructive here. When I say destruction of collective memory, I don't mean the emergence of separate partial memories, the Oriental [Mizrahi] memory, or the Palestinian memory or the female memory, or the memory of sexual minorities. I have no problems with these and other minorities, no, the more memories the better. What worries me is the total erosion of all the collective memories, all of them. And in favor of what? According to a graffiti I saw the other day on the road from Arad: *We were born to shop.* This is instead of the entire hard disc. Now, I cannot reconstruct the whole hard disc, but I wanted to make a diskette, a family diskette to give to my children. They use it or they don't use it, as they wish, but I have left them a diskette and I've put on it what I could, to some extent in an apologetic way, saying to them: Look. And now I'm quoting Galia, my youngest daughter, because in some way what she said meant the most to me—"Everyone here is a refugee and a holocaust survivor, even the Mizrahim"—she said this after reading a page of *A Tale of Love and Darkness,*—"this whole country is a refugee camp." This is an insight that should have been evident to everyone, either from the textbooks, or from the ceremonies, from Yom Ha'atzmaut [Independence Day], or Yom Hazikharon [Remembrance Day], or Yom Hashoah [Holocaust Memorial Day]—it's everywhere, all the time, and yet it is not. It is erased. It is even erased from the political and international and internal debate. This country is a refugee camp and this country was a life-saving port for people who otherwise would have been dead. Now, in terms of human history six million murdered Jews or six and a half million murdered Jews would not make a huge difference to mankind. But half a million Jews who found a life-saving raft here would have otherwise been murdered. I'm talking about the half a million European and local Jews who otherwise would have been murdered. This is something of which I am very much aware. But being a refugee country is not only a tragedy; it is also a comedy.

G.S.: This issue is very important to me. I have just finished writing a book entitled, Identity, *on Jewish writers, and in it I quote a talk I gave at Ben Gurion University where I said, at some point, that the Holocaust has had a greater influence on the Israeli experience than any other event. A young professor stood up and said, "That's not true. The Holocaust is only a justification for the occupation." That's how I end my book.*

Oz: The love-hate relationship with the old country is the same as with my parents. That's why Sami Michael's *Victoria* is so similar to East European Jewish novels.

G.S.: With out a doubt, Victoria *is a novel about the old country. And it's an "Eastern" novel in two senses: East European and Mizrahi. But let's go on. You said this book was intended for your children and grandchildren yet it effected many other readers. [Literary scholar] Yigal Schwartz read readers' letters to you and wrote an essay presenting them as worshipers and you as a literary priest. Did you find this title flattering? A burden? How did you feel about the reception of this novel?*

Oz: I was totally surprised by the reception, and not just by this title. I had said to my wife: this book is going to be read by very few people. It's going to be read by people who are either from the same village or the same vintage, or both. And very few others. And indeed when I presented it to the publisher—to Keter—they panicked. They said, we cannot sell this book, it is a book for people who are part of the story and no one else. That it was so broadly received came to me as a total surprise. Now, what Yigal [Schwartz]—says, that it is a cult book—this is true for a very limited number of people who are really from the same village, same vintage. For most readers—and now in many other countries, because it has of course been translated—it's about them wanting to tell me *their* stories. Most of the letters I get are not cult letters, but letters from people who say: all right, I've heard your story, now you hear mine (and sometimes at length). But what I'm beginning to understand now is this: that the guiding principle of the novel is this combination of the very intimate chamber music of the family with the broad historical scene, not as a remote background but as part of the story. Much greater writers than myself have done the same. Tolstoy did it in *War and Peace* and Lampedusa in *The Leopard*, and the wonderful Italian author Elsa Morante in *La Storia*. The same marriage of an intimate family tale interwoven with a history book, with literature, values—viewed from a certain distance, viewed as if it is coming to an end, as if it is no longer here, viewed with the cool eye of someone who is no longer part of it, is not nostalgic about it, but not in the business of killing it either.

G.S.: You and your generation of writers, who were referred to as the "new wave" during the 60s and 70s, are now the fathers' generation. You are now in the position of Moshe Shamir, S. Yizhar, Aharon Megged, Nathan Shaham and all the other writers who, according to your book, sat in the cafés, and you [your generation] did not like them. You are now in the same situation: writers sit at home and say, "there is the left-ist mafia of Oz, A.B. Yehoshua, and so on." The rebellion against your generation is not political—Etgar Keret and Zeruya Shalev are no less "left" than you are. This is a rebellion about themes, about a different style. You now have perspective. We are compiling this issue of MHL on love in postmodern times. What do you make of this generation, some of them younger than your own children?

Oz: There are about half a dozen brilliant talents, writers who have the tools, the language, the wit and sometimes a lightness that makes me envy them. One or two dance where I can only walk—I don't want to name names—and I envy their ability to dance. They probably envy me, and my intimate relationship with history, even though they pretend not to envy it at all. I have some kind of personal contact with that which for them is impersonal, and therefore—for many of them—also very alien and frightening. I don't blame them for this. But I blame them at times for something else (and this is a fairly angry accusation): lack of curiosity. I regard lack of curiosity as an esthetic flaw in an artist, and a moral flaw in a human being. I don't expect anyone to love my generation or my political party or my political ideas. I don't expect anyone to love anyone at all. This "who loves who" is none of my business. But I do expect people to be curious, even about those they don't like, and in much of the literature that is being written today I find an almost deliberate lack of curiosity about former generations, about other corners of the present. Tel Aviv literature seems to be totally uninterested in anything outside Tel Aviv. Ultra-Orthodox and Orthodox literature seem to lack any curiosity, except for Orthodox people who have become secular. They show a total lack of curiosity about the spirituality of those who are not orthodox. In fact, they tend to deny its existence. Sensuality yes, *bon vivance* yes, but spirituality—no. This, in my view, is both an esthetic flaw and a moral sin. Not only for writers, for people altogether. Not to be curious is a sin, I don't mean a major sin—you don't execute people for not being curious. Being curious has to do with imagining the other, and by the other I don't necessarily mean the trendy other: the Palestinian, the oriental [Jew], the female, the homosexual, no. Imagining the other is sometimes imagining the kid next door, or your parent, or your child or your mate. This is missing. You know, in a strange way I found the same flaw in the previous generation of writers, of the 1940s and 1950s. In many of them there was a similar flaw, a kind of lack of curiosity about anything apart from the camp fire and the kibbutz and the Haganah and dancing the hora, with exceptions [like Yehudit] Hendel. She was an outstanding exception in that generation. There were others, but not many.

G.S.: What you are saying is that the young writers of today are returning to "Tamid Anachnu" ["Always Us," the Palmach anthem], but Nathan Shaham has gone in different directions in his latest novels. You claim that our young authors suffer from mental provincialism.

Oz: Yes, indeed. I know what you're talking about. Many of them are very cosmopolitan [only because] they write with New York in mind. I'm going to make a further claim, beyond what you said about mental provincialism: anyone who can write *only* about him- or herself cannot really write about that self either, because no man is an island. And I mean this not only as a metaphor. No one of us is an island. Not one of us begin on the date that is registered in our birth certificate, and not one of us is just born where he was born, in the city or the town where he was made. A writer, a poet, a story-teller, a novelist, a dramatist who writes only about himself or herself cannot even write properly about that. At the same time, you have a different kind of provincialism: "internationalism," people who write books which are meant to be broadly received by international audiences. I've been very pampered by international audiences—I don't complain and I don't have reason to envy anyone. But I have a secret to share with some of those younger writers: the more provincial, the more parochial and local a novel is, the better chance it stands of becoming universal. Universal is not international. International novels are a different business. They are bought in international hotels and airports, people read them on international flights and then they leave them on a bench at an international airport. They live and die inside the international ghetto, they never leave it, whereas some truly provincial works travel very far, because of this human need to compare. How do those very strange people on the other side of the universe live? Are they exactly like me, are they totally different, are they both like me and different? This is something which I wish I could teach.

G.S.: I have been told that Latin American literature and Hebrew litera-ture arouse the most interest in Europe today, mainly because they are so-called provincial, but are actually universal. Tolstoy was very provincial.

Oz: And Faulkner and Chekhov…

G.S.: When I think of your generation, I think of five major names: Yehuda Amichai, A.B. Yehoshua, Amalia Kahana-Carmon, Aharon Appelfeld and you. If I ask myself whether there are five such names today. Well, many of the young writers seem so similar. What do you think?

Oz: Let's be fair. If you look at *Keshet* [a leading literary journal] in the 1960s, with seven or eight short stories or novellas in each issue, you will find that many of the issues suffer from the same syndrome: you could stop in the middle [of a story] and read the next one, and not even notice the difference. It was like that in the 60s, and the same in the 40s. The difference is that we have three, maybe five names left from the 40s and the rest are gone. From the 60s it's similar, although some of those who have disappeared deserve not to be forgotten. But still, there was an ocean of novels and stories, perhaps not in the same numbers as now because the market is bigger and the business is bigger. But there was an ocean of books whose authors—I don't want to name names but you know who I'm talking about—wrote novels and published them, and the novels were reviewed and they were interchangeable. You could stop one in the middle and move on to the next one. The difference now lies in you and me, Gershon. I'll tell you what: our senses were sharper about the literature of the 50s and 60s, we were better readers of the previous generation than of our own. I remind myself [of this] in moments of anger. Sometimes I get very angry at what I read. Then I remind myself, I say: Amos be careful, remember this old man Menachem Dorman [critic and editor] who at some point said that I no longer understand, it's no longer my world. Maybe it's wonderful, but it's no longer my world. At some point this will be true about me and you. Maybe not quite yet, but some of it is already there. There may be things which are brilliant and I don't get them. You know how I know it? Music. Certain kinds of music which, I presume, are powerful and meaningful and deep, are meaningless to me not because of their quality but because of me. I don't want to become one of those silly old men who think that the world has to stop with their cognition.

G.S.: Let me quote our teacher Dov Sadan who wrote a wonderful essay on you...

Oz: "The Sides of the Mountain." He was a very smart man—in that article he predicted *A Tale of Love and Darkness.*

G.S.: Once, when he had to give a prize for a first book of poems, he asked me to bring him something new. I brought him [Yehuda] Amichai's first book, and he said, "Look, his Hebrew is not my Hebrew, but I trust you. I don't understand any poetry after [Nathan] Alterman. It's not about them, it's about me. Since you are younger than me, I'm glad you can still find authors that you admire today.

Oz: Not only admire but envy, as I have said before.

G.S.: You are one of the last writers to use a Hebrew that is rich. What do you think, in terms of our cultural context, of the fact that Hebrew books are growing away from the cultural canon, and becoming closer not only to spoken language, but to what I call "sub-language"—slang?

Oz: First of all, I'm utterly biased. I'm not objective, because when it comes to Hebrew I'm a hopeless chauvinist. I'm not a chauvinist for the country—I love my country even when I don't like it. I love Israel even when I cannot stand it, but I'm not a chauvinist. When it comes to Hebrew, I'm an excited chauvinist, a groupie of the Hebrew language. This is my musical instrument, this is my life, so I cannot talk about it in a scholarly way. Now I'll tell you this: for me, Hebrew is a very rich orchestra with some very archaic musical instruments, like the harpsichord, and some very contemporary ones. I went through a time in my writing life, when I tried to stick to the more traditional layers of Hebrew because they attracted me more. No longer. Now I feel a sense of kinship towards the entire spectrum of the language except for deliberately bastardized English that is disguised as Hebrew. But other than that, when I write I do not hesitate to use a harpsichord next to a mouth organ next to an electric synthesizer. I may use all of them depending on what I want to do on a given page, in a given scene.

I think Hebrew is confronting a deadly danger. And I think that this is much more serious than any other so called demographic or cultural threat, because we if we lose our language, we will lose the only common denominator of our many identities. This is a common denominator which we have created not through ideology but through necessity. And let us not forget that spoken Hebrew was revived, not because Ben Yehuda was persistent and a genius, and not because the pioneers were very ideological and committed to Hebrew. It was revived because the Ashkenazi influx of immigrants and the indigenous Sephardi population in Jerusalem had no other language in common. For an immigrant, for an Orthodox Jew from Hungary or Poland who came to Jerusalem, the only way to ask directions to the Wailing Wall, or to rent a room, or to rent a business was to apply to prayer book Hebrew. There was no other common language. I can tell you the exact moment when Hebrew became a living language after seventeen centuries of hibernation. It became a living language the moment a boy whispered to a girl, or a girl to a boy, "I love you," in Hebrew. Because for seventeen centuries it was not used in intimate circumstances. Yes, [it was used] around the *Seder*-night table or in the synagogue or in rabbinical negotiations, or even in literary periodicals and magazines from the 18th century on, and in poetry in Spain. But not in the bedroom. No one in bed spoke Hebrew. No Jew spoke Hebrew to another Jew in bed for seventeen centuries. When this boy whispered to that girl or the girl to the boy, "I love you"—this was the moment of revival. It happened in Jerusalem at the end of the 19th century, just a hundred and fifty years ago or so. And it happened because the boy was Ashkenazi and girl Sephardi or vice versa, and there was no other way for the two of them. This is how it was revived, let's not forget it. But it could just have been an episode, come and go, disappear. After a few years, either the immigrants would learn to speak Ladino, or if they outnumbered the locals, the locals would learn Yiddish. The fact that it kept on going was because there was a waiting, ready body of modern literature, with modern sensibilities, and modern senses and a modern sense of the world, ready and waiting for several decades. This was amazing, and it is something I don't understand, even after reading your book on the history of Hebrew prose between the 1880s and the 1980s. I don't understand how people who never spoke Hebrew in everyday life could write mimetic novels in Hebrew. For poetry, I can understand, even allegorical drama I understand, but trying to create mimetic prose—and I mean Mendele—how could a man who never spoke Hebrew try to create or imitate a dialogue in broken Hebrew, a dialogue between simple people, a dialogue between artisans, or between Benjamin and Sendrel [from Mendele's *The Travels of Benjamin the Third*] in Hebrew? To me, this is not only a mystery, but also the deep explanation of how the revival of Hebrew could be more than just a short episode. You know, it's a miracle! I'm getting carried away, I can't stop when I talk about Hebrew.

When I was seven years old, there were no more than four hundred thousand people worldwide who spoke Hebrew in their everyday life, most of them here. In Jerusalem when I was a boy, anyone who was over forty-five spoke other languages, so much so that I feared that when I grew up and turned forty-five, I would wake up one morning speaking Yiddish—like graying hair, like wrinkles, it was something that came with age. Four hundred thousand from a few thousand at the beginning of the 20th century, and today to seven million people. Do you know that seven million people speak Hebrew every day now? In Israel, in the occupied territories, in Europe, in America—seven million people! Not all of them Israeli citizens, not all of them Jews. Seven million people is more than the number of Norwegian speakers worldwide, it is more than the number of Danish speakers worldwide, it is more than the number of English speakers worldwide in the days of William Shakespeare, because in the days of Shakespeare there were, on both sides of the ocean, no more than four to five million English speakers, that was all. To me, the fact that today, people speaking this language fly jumbo jets, conduct open heart surgery and launch satellites into orbit... I respond like a little child each time I think about it! And that's why the attempt to flatten it, to bastardize it, to mock it and make fun of it, to destroy, not the vocabulary—I don't care about the vocabulary, that has always been bastardized—but the deep structure of the language, the logic and the ethic of the language, this I regard as a deadly danger. But I'm not objective.

G.S.: One last question, which is actually an introduction to this issue of MHL: *love in Hebrew literature, once dominated by shyness, today by the lack of it. I read stories today, most of them by women, where there is hardly any Eros, just sex. I'd like to hear your opinion of the literary construction of love here and now.*

Oz: I cannot speak about love in English, so I will answer this last question in Hebrew![1] First of all, it is very difficult to write about

---

1. The rest of this interview was conducted in English.

love, not only here but in general, because to write about love is like drawing a sunset or a vase filled with flowers. All the great masters have already done it. What can one write about love after the Song of Songs, Petrarch and Shakespeare? So first of all, it's difficult. Second, for us, in secular Israeli culture, the period of love was very short. There was a time when people produced entire floods of emotion so as not to write about eroticism. Today, it's easier for two young people to get into bed than to write each other love letters—if you give them a choice—because it's hard to write a love letter. So actually, love for us had a very short blossoming period between the puritan age and age of sexual inflation. It began with Agnon and Lea Goldberg, he in prose, and she in poetry… and maybe also Gnessin. It ends more or less with David Grossman and Meir Shalev. You will not find many people who write about love today—they write about loneliness and the absence of love. You could say, of course, that writing about the absence of love is also writing about love, but the amazing thing is that in the most promiscuous environment you find people who go back and ask Bialik's question—"They say there is love in the world. What is love?" As though we had come a full circle. I would be very happy to live longer and witness the return of love—she'll return, she's a stubborn creature. Yet love's moment in modern Hebrew literature and Hebrew life was very short, a short spring that has come and gone.

July 7, 2005

Poetry

RONNY SOMECK was born in Baghdad, Iraq, in 1951, and arrived in Israel two years later. He studied Hebrew literature and philosophy at Tel Aviv University and drawing at the Avni Academy of Art. In addition to working as a counselor with street gangs, Someck teaches literature and holds writing workshops. A leading Israeli poet, Someck began publishing in 1968. His publications include eight books of poetry and a book for children which he co-authored with his daughter, Shirly. In 1997, he recorded a CD, *Revenge of the Stuttering Child*, with musician Elliot Sharp in New York. In 1998, Someck and artist Benny Efrat had a joint exhibition entitled "Nature's Factory" at the Israel Museum. Someck has received the ACUM Special Jubilee Prize, the Prime Minister's Prize and the Amichai Prize (2004). His poetry has been translated into six languages.

The poems are from Someck's collection, *The Milk Underground*, Tel Aviv, Zmora Bitan, 2005. 48 pp.

Ronny Someck

Three Poems

COURTING

Y. asks my daughter to go steady. She's nine and half years old.
He's two months older. That's the combined age
in whose honor a poet like Jacques Prévert dimmed the lights of
Paris.
But here, in Ramat Gan, the batteries barely suffice
for the back of a firefly shedding light on hearts
scribbled in the margins of a torn page.
So here you are, Innocence, a bag of sugar ripped open
and sprinkled on stolen dough to knead
with sticky fingers a cake
that sweetens a new shelf
in the pastry-shop of the body.

ONE-MAN MAFIA

When the moon lays on the windowsill
the bags of light it stole from the sun,

Ronny Someck

we bribe our limbs from head to toe,
pilfer diamonds of sweat,
gather a handful of each other
and curl up at the end of the bed like a one-man
mafia.

SPRINKLER

for Liora and Shirly

Love erupts in thin jets
from the sprinkler's pinholes.
We too, like the earth's cheek,
thirst for the water's kiss.

Translated from the Hebrew by Gabriel Levin

MAYA BEJERANO was born at Kibbutz Elon in 1949, spent her childhood in Jaffa and now lives in Tel Aviv. Bejerano holds a BA in literature and philosophy from Bar Ilan University, has studied violin and flute and is an amateur photographer. She has an MA in library science from the Hebrew University of Jerusalem and works as consultant at the Tel Aviv Municipal Library. Bejerano has published nine books of poetry. She has been awarded the Prime Minister's Prize, the Bialik Prize (2002), and the Bernstein Prize (1989). Her poetry has been published in 12 languages.

The poems are from Bejerano's collection, *Frequencies: Selected Poems 1978–2004*, Tel Aviv, Hakibbutz Hameuchad, 2005. 424 pp.

Maya Bejerano

Three Poems

FALLING IN LOVE WITH MYSELF THROUGH
ANOTHER

for M. Geldman

Tonight her eyes flashed with the spark
of sapphires toward me
but before I made note of it
I lingered in her spell
as she recited my poem in her voice—
naturally, in whose voice could she have read
the poem if not her own?
Perhaps another's voice joined hers,
magnifying the sparkling allure of her glance
as she read my poem
the dark green dress enveloping her
stirring like sea velvet
enhancing her charm.
I said velvet, let me add foam
ascribed to the delectable glow of her cheek
fused with the stinging saltiness of sea froth
sickening and healing at once

and the scent of dense grasses
from a distant land.

I know that when the night ends—
I'll kiss her.

A MINUTE GARDEN OF EDEN

A minute Garden of Eden in the recess of my head,
so identified during a hurried drive, through the quite heavy traffic,
toward a specific location in town, more precisely,
outside town, but not too far beyond it.
What was it that in such a minute space of time
flickered like a pulse of light from dim distances—
a beam of thought that binds all particles of my being,
no pain getting in the way, just the complete body,
seated, relaxed, absorbing the simple shifting of gears
on a rain-soaked thoroughfare
on either side tidy flowers and intra-city lawns
signs testifying to the known identity of place
and yet—not a negligible everyday detail
underneath the surface your attention is drawn inward
as you maneuver the profusion of overpasses,
the route as basic as the specific destination—
not for me, but for the dear one I am driving.
Briefly, a new vision forms,
a glance into my innermost that has fallen from my eyes
to the hidden satisfying place identified
as my inviolable Garden of Eden
my own Garden of Eden
secreted and found.

THE HANDS OF AUTUMN

The deluding seducing warmth of autumn
is short,
disrobing like a fashionable hanger dress;
and the nerves of the city all around,
arching threads in mourning,
growing gray against a pinkish, darkening backdrop,
then vanishing in the evening.
Narrow handcuffs close on the loud
blue heart, and beyond,
the sea drops and hides,
facing a sea of blue air above.
And I fancy myself as the white
quivering flesh of the oyster,
lying on a stone bench,
an earth basket,
reflected in the eyes of a glorious god
as I diminish
in the hands of time

Translated from the Hebrew by Tsipi Keller

ISRAEL PINCAS was born in Sofia, Bulgaria, in 1935, and immi-grated to Israel as a child. He currently divides his time between Tel Aviv and Paris. Pincas has worked as night editor for United Press, as translator, and as editor at Am Oved and Sifriat Poalim Publish-ing Houses. He has also managed two art galleries and continues to work with contemporary art. Pincas began publishing poetry in 1951. He has received several literary awards, including the Bernstein Prize (1981), the Prime Minister's Prize and, most recently, the prestigious Israel Prize for literature (2005). His poetry has been translated into 15 languages.

The poems in this selection are from Pincas' collection *Discourse on Time: Poems 1979–1989*, Tel Aviv, Hakibbutz Hameuchad, 1991. 141 pp.

Israel Pincas

Three Poems

SCRIPT

When love was here, on her royal visit,
she brought such splendor that many,
as though operated from within,
sensed her presence,
until she veiled herself like mist, completely.
Astonished, we spoke of it to others.
Is it any wonder
That so little remained?
Will the scribes and magi of our lives,
with such meager data in hand,
work out something of our ancient script?

But we, whom love traversed
and turned over like flowerbeds,
understood what had happened and therefore,
silent and withdrawn,
folded the black canvas sheets
of our crooked tents, the ropes and pelts,
the leftovers of our crass meal, the narrow

means of easing our pains,
and unknowingly began to trace
foreign and complicated shapes in the sand.

Now, when dusk raises
an image stricken and cold,
and within the ridiculous, unavoidable
tumult and noise
that the dimmed body creates,
each one sees how we must
concentrate and think of her,
of the smallest details of her being,
her fading face, her appearance, the hem
of her dress, so that
should she call on our realm again,
her splendor won't singe
the thin, white wings
we imagined in her absence rising within us,
and which we are surprised to discover,
so that her light might burn our eyes less,
and we'll be able, perhaps, in all our humbleness
from this desert, for once to rise.

Translated from the Hebrew by Gabriel Levin

THE RAIN   *in memory of Efrat Ofek*

The rain which falls on me this year is certainly no different
from the rain of past years: brown and aggressive, matter of fact,
red sometimes,
in Tel Aviv and in the Upper Galilee and in Rome,
hotter the more south you go,

or soft and grey, hesitating, tiny like crying,
in London and in Paris,
almost not felt in the countries of the north,

but the rain which falls sometimes on a twenty and thirty year old,
on a forty year old,
finds me today as one who passed through these
years, as one who these years passed over,
and from this standpoint it is therefore different rain, which falls on
another person and
place, and at a different time.

Again I do not hear its bluish, hypnotic speech—a sign
of the expansion of the time—
as I once heard in Stratford,
or at home with the parrot, the home of the widow of the naval
officer—in Earl's Court—
also didn't hear his fiery speech that awakens to renewal

and growth; the rain that begins to fall at night in the north
and spreads
now on the entire face of the coastal plain,
which wets the lupin valley in the Galilee and the orange
tulips, which once startled me by the entrance to the cosmos,
graves of young people,

this rain does not resemble any rain which I have known.
It is almost without color;
its speech isn't hinted at again like once,
in fact it resembles silence more,

on its way as if trying to tell me
I don't have much time here,
that I must hurry and arrange my affairs
my many matters, just when I don't have any interest in a journey,

when I feel that I am not entirely ready.

Afterwards the rains of old age will come,
accompanied by winds changing direction,
the monsoon of the body,
after them another rain
white perhaps, neutral, without name.

THE STATE

It was in May.
I loved a girl then. Her name was

Vali.
I remember her because she sat

in front of me in class, because she had a braid and she
laughed a lot and her clothes and her notebooks

were always neat and clean.
One Sabbath we took a trip to the Seven Mills

She prepared cold juice, sandwiches wrapped in wax paper and
cookies

and fruit. I tried to kiss her and she
slapped me.

Several months later I learned of the partition
plan.

The state was established. It awoke as if from a deep
sleep.

My uncle woke me in the middle of the night
after he heard the news from Lake Success,

he yelled at me in great emotion
and gave me ten pennies.

Aside from that, after the establishment of the state,
I didn't have much success.

Translated from the Hebrew by Linda Zisquit

Review Essay

Gershon Shaked

Jephthah's Daughter

Yoram Kaniuk, *His Daughter*, 1987
Tel Aviv, Yedioth Ahronoth, 2004. 319 pp.

In his novel, *His Daughter*, first published in 1987 and recently reissued, Kaniuk deals with a complex subject: the burden of guilt borne by the fathers—the winners of the War of Independence and subsequent wars—precisely because of their victory. It is victory that turned the former victims of the Holocaust into the source of victimization of today's helpless refugees. And since these fathers have not atoned for their misdeeds, their sons take on the burden of responsibility and punish themselves in their stead. In this book, Kaniuk gives the myth of guilt—which also underlies S. Yizhar's novella, *Hirbet Hiz'ah*—its most radical expression.

His Daughter is written as the confession of the central character, Joseph Krieger, and this technique creates the effect of non-fictional art. The manuscript is given to a publisher by Asa who, as witness-narrator, confirms its authenticity.

> In these pages, I appear as a frustrated writer, the one who was Miriam Hurwitz's husband and enemy. But the sorrow over her death cannot hide the fact that Krieger, in his youth, and I all my life, from the time I was nineteen, both loved the same mysterious macabre

woman, a touch of whose character emerges, perhaps, in her namesake, Krieger's daughter, Miriam, who in so tragic a fashion was forcibly driven by the cruel inevitability of death's wheel and died inside a house which the army had destroyed in retaliation against terrorist activity in the area around village K. in the district of Tulkarem.

The novel starts out as a mystery bordering on fantasy, continues as a novel of quest and intrigue, and concludes as a confession. Three men have been friends since their army days: Reuben, who becomes head of the Mossad, the Chief of Staff and Joseph Krieger, an officer who took part in reprisal raids and fought in all the wars. All three were in love with Miriam, a nurse in the War of Independence (she is also the heroine of Kaniuk's *Himmo, King of Jerusalem*, which creates an interesting intertextual connection between the two works). Subsequently, all three fall in love with a young Holocaust survivor, the beautiful Nina, a *femme fatale* who married Joseph and is having a love affair with Reuben.

The central plot describes Joseph's search for his daughter, Miriam, who has disappeared. The head of the Mossad, the Chief of Staff and the police officer are also involved in the search, and as suspicions concerning the cause of her disappearance shift from person to person, the narrative describes the changing relationship between three friends. Only towards the end is the body discovered, and it then transpires that her death is connected to that of Isaac, a young soldier who was killed in a reprisal raid commanded by Joseph, and for which Isaac's family hold him responsible.

Like in several of Kaniuk's other novels, the melodramatic entanglement creates a sequence, which enables him to include various philosophical and expressionist interludes.

Thematically, the novel focuses on the Jewish-Arab conflict: it opens and closes with it. As the narrative unfolds, we reach the moment of sin that drives the plot: during a reprisal raid, an Arab home is burned to the ground and Isaac, who opposes such raids, is killed when he tries to rescue an old woman although Joseph, his commanding officer, tries to save him. Aware of her father's "sin," Miriam falls in love with the dead youth, and her entire life is marked by the tension between her living father and the dead soldier. She in turn dies—like Isaac—when she goes into an Arab house scheduled for destruction and is buried under the ruins. Thus she takes on her father's sin and its punishment, punishing him in turn through her death. Ultimately, Joseph attempts suicide and toward the end of the novel, he is either in a coma or dying.

The characters in this novel represent various social groups. Joseph is the good soldier dedicated to serving the state; Nina is a half-Jewish Holocaust survivor. Miriam is torn between her father and mother, and between her father's role in the military and the outlook of Isaac—as well as his younger brother—who totally reject the war of the Jews against the Arabs. On another level, the conflict between father, mother and daughter is destructive in its own right, and this family dynamic and is one of the sources of the conflict.

One may assume that the author was thinking in general sociological categories: the three officers represent the "new Hebrew" who is fascinated by and drawn to the "old" Jew, represented by Nina, the refugee. Thus, on a symbolic level, the fathers in this family are "new Hebrews" while the mothers are "old Jews." Miriam is torn between the two poles but is closer to her mother and to the pacifist (Jewish) Isaac, who refuses to be a "new Hebrew,"—synonymous, for Kaniuk, with warriors and conquerors. The rift leads to ruin and suicide, and for this reason *His Daughter* is mainly about guilt—it is guilt that draws Miriam to the particular house (or one like it) where Isaac was killed and where she too loses her life. Symbolically, she is the daughter of Jephthah, but she is also Iphigenia: both the innocent victim and the price her father pays for Israeli aggression. She identifies with her mother, who is also a victim—in her case, of Nazi persecution—and she denounces her father in the letters she sends him before her death-suicide. In fact, she rejects him precisely because she sees him as the "ideal Israeli," the so-called virtuous soldier. She hates these qualities, which she views as faults. In her eyes, the pacifist Isaac and Holocaust survivors like Nina are the oxymoronic antithesis—the "negative" as it were—of the "new Hebrew," who is the "positive." Nina herself presents this opposition in a paradoxical but clear way:

> Here you are Sabras, you have falafel with pita, heat-waves. You don't grasp the nightmares we brought here with us. Miriam is grafted on two trees. One branch is old and rotten, but beautiful; the other is young and healthy, but ugly, utterly unappealing.

In other words, it is Nina's self-negation that leads her to see the opposite pole as negative. The plot that leads from Isaac's death to Miriam's suicide is intended to refute the Zionist metaplot. Victory over the Arabs does not lead to redemption, for the young refuse to be the "silver platter" on which—to paraphrase Natan Alterman—the Jewish state was served up. They anticipate, not victory and redemption but the possibility of destruction and loss. As Miriam says to her father:

> [When you] got into shape to fight Arabs, you never grasped how deeply justified the Arabs felt. I may not accept their sense of justice—I'm incapable of that and must agree with you—but I can at least understand it; they opposed Jewish immigration not out of animosity to mother. They said, "It's our land, in ruins, desolate, but ours; let the enlightened world find another place for the refugees." In the end, yes, only a few refugees were left, and they had lost their own lands. Up to this point everything makes sense, but once you go beyond it towards your extreme self-justification you become if not fanatic, color-blind. How did Isaac Raphaeli put it? You'll never have enough bullets to kill off a hundred million Arabs, and since his death you must add on another hundred million.
>
> Why do you think they were obliged to under-stand the intense suffering of all the Ninas? Who gave you permission to speak on behalf of all those Ninas?

As a novel about the sin, guilt and punishment of both the sacrificed daughter and the sacrificing father (Jephthah who kills himself after his daughter is sacrificed on the altar of war), *My Daughter* is a subversive account of the erosion of Zionist "justice."

Reviews

Flawed Identity

Aharon Appelfeld, *Poland, a Green Country*
Jerusalem, Keter, 2005. 217 pp.

True, Poland is a green country covered in dense forests and wide fields, but it is also the largest cemetery of the Jewish people. Israelis go there to visit death camps and Jewish sites where time stands still. Apparently, thousands of us also crowd around the gates of the Polish Embassy in order to apply for Polish citizenship. If our enemies should rise up to destroy us or, Heaven forbid, some other calamity, these people will be able to find shelter in Europe thanks to their Polish passports.

The main character in Aharon Appelfeld's new novel also sets out on a personal quest to Poland, but of a different sort. He returns there in order to connect to his lost Jewish identity, even though he was not born in Poland, and has always rejected the qualities it represents. Unlike Appelfeld's previous heroes who were born in Europe, Yaakov Fein is an Israeli, born in Tel Aviv to Holocaust survivors. He has done everything possible to dissociate himself from the world of his parents, who were born in a small village near Cracow and could never erase the terrible memories of their childhood.

In Appelfeld's opinion, Israeli identity is a flawed identity, and he expresses this through his main character. Yaakov Fein is a typical sabra (native-born Israeli); he was a member of the Hashomer Hatzair left-wing youth movement, completed his army service with the rank of captain and is attracted to kibbutz-born women, who used to represent the best of Israel. He first revolted against his Jewish past when he refused to have a bar mitzvah; later, after his parents' death, he sold their house and all its contents, leaving no trace of them. He also converted the textile store he inherited into a successful fashion boutique. But Fein is not a happy man. His Israeli identity does not satisfy his spiritual needs, and he has misgivings about his cold, pragmatic wife and his daughters who resemble her. As we can see from his attitude towards them, his new family is also flawed, and his journey to Poland is intended to correct all these flaws.

It seems to me no accident that Appelfeld has chosen Poland this time rather than Austro-Hungarian Bukovina—where he lived as child—because, more than anywhere else, Poland symbolizes the deeply rooted Jewish world that has disappeared for ever. And indeed, it is the antithesis of the rootless Israeli existence. According to Appelfeld, all those who were raised on the Zionist revolution and have renounced their Judaism are in fact assimilationists, and the reader is asked to note the similarities between Yaakov and his Aunt Bronka who became a communist, as well as his Uncle Leshek, who converted to Christianity. They were both lost to the Jewish people, while Yaakov is trying to return to his roots and redefine himself as a Jew. "Are the Israelis Jews?" asks the taxi driver who drives Yaakov to his parents' village, Szirovza. "Jews," Yaakov replies and he is clearly referring to more than just the nationality recorded in his passport.

But can one return to a lost Eden? As in Appelfeld's other books (*The Age of Wonders*, for example) it is a late return to Europe, and Yaakov pays only a fleeting visit to his parents' village. There is nothing there, people tell him, dismissing the remote village. At the end of his search, Yaakov will come to the same conclusion: to a certain extent, Szirovza is located outside of history, a green but illusory village. Initially, he rediscovers Jewish memory in the shape of Magda, a Polish woman who, as a child, was a frequent visitor to his grandparents' home. She sings him the Yiddish lullaby "*Rozhinkes mit mandlen*" ("Raisins and Almonds"), and serves him the dishes his mother used to cook. Magda is older than Yaakov but she looks young, full of vitality and she acts as a substitute for mother and wife—when Yaakov sleeps with her, he is connected to his family and his roots. But just as the village preserves Jewish memory, it also preserves its hatred and fear of Jews, which it directs against Yaakov. Clearly, this

Eden is the same hell where the Jews of Szirovza were locked in the synagogue by their Polish neighbors and burnt alive.

Ultimately, as Yaakov realizes, Jewishness is not a physical place but a place of the soul. Leaving behind his grandfather's gravestone, he returns to his family in Israel, filled with concern for his sick daughter. At the end of the cathartic journey, the son has become a father.

Poland, a Green Country, is a fascinating and relevant novel. Personally, I was moved to tears.

Haya Hoffman

All-Conquering Conflict

Sami Michael, *Pigeons in Trafalgar Square*
Tel Aviv, Am Oved, 2005. 215 pp.

In the main, literature has not dealt with the Israeli-Palestinian conflict in the last few years. Although it frequently serves as a backdrop, only a few Israeli writers meet this conflict head-on and delve into its complexity. Sami Michael does.

The novel starts with an event that occurred in Haifa during the confusion of the War of Independence. In the tide of Arabs fleeing the city, an Arab woman is separated from her baby which is left alone in the house. A childless Holocaust survivor who moves into the house finds it and raises it as her own. Thus Badir, the Arab baby, becomes the Jew Ze'ev Epstein who grows up not as the son of Nabila the refugee, but as the son of Riva, the refugee who has found her place. On this foundation, Michael builds a human story full of twists of fate, and portrays the lives of both protagonists as well as the development of the conflict from both sides.

When Ze'ev grows up, he discovers the truth about his origins. He and Nabila grow very close, and he also forms relationships with his biological family. However, he has no father. His adoptive father died when he was eight, in the Sinai Campaign, and when he meets his biological family ten years later—they are now refugees living in the occupied West Bank—his father is very hostile and regards him as an enemy. But Ze'ev does have a kind of father: Shmiel, a man who courted Riva when they were still "there," before the Holocaust, and who later becomes close to the "stuck together" family living in the abandoned Arab house, even though he does not win Riva.

The novel can be read on two levels. On the human level, it is a complicated, painful story, often obscure and enigmatic, sometimes melodramatic and yet endlessly amazing. Slices of real life—almost impossible, one thinks at times—that no fiction can surpass. The second level is the way Michael presents the conflict between the two peoples, and here too his sense of proportion is unwavering. A particularly sensitive point is the symmetry that every hasty hand rushes to depict: Holocaust/*Naqba*, Occupation/Hamas, "preventive assassination"/"*amaliyyeh istashahadiyyeh*" (or "suicide bombing," according to that side of the conflict). Here too, Michael makes generous use of his knowledge of both sides in depicting the mental and cultural dynamics of each of the rival sides; it is also evident when he characterizes the tremendous difficulty of every encounter, both emotionally and on the level of "security coordination" and "understandings between the parties." Throughout the novel, the complex personal-family plot develops through stages of pain and sudden mental change, but the most remarkable is Michael's sharp, terse characterization of "the situation."

Sami Michael's book leaves us with clear but depressing conclusions about the Israeli-Palestinian conflict. Both peoples are locked in a killing embrace, like villagers living on the slopes of a volcano.

Ioram Melcer

The Old Man and the Satire

Aharon Megged, *The Honeymoons of Professor Lunz*
Tel Aviv, Zmora Bitan, 2005. 155 pp.

Lunz, a professor of Ancient Eastern Studies, joins the long line of Aharon Megged's scholarly protagonists. Megged has added him to his list of literature professors (*Evyatar's Notebooks*), literary critics (*The Flying Camel and the Golden Hump*), and translators (*Yotam's Vengeance*) in order to grapple once again with the burning issues of Israeli society. At the age of 73, Lunz shocks his acquaintances when he suddenly divorces his wife, the mother of his children, and marries Ayala, a student fifty years his junior. Yoav, the professor's assistant, witnesses the turmoil in the Lunz home, the fleeting happiness enjoyed by the strange couple, the eccentric professor's loss of sanity and his death. Yoav also provides the narrative framework for the story—a favored practice of Megged's—and we follow his repeated mood swings from reverence to contempt as he types up his mentor's essays on the Emorites, whom Lunz claims to be the ancestors of the Jewish people. Yoav is also erotically attracted to his mentor's wife, a mysterious girl with a passionate love for life who is drawn to healers and fortune tellers. She tells him a little about her marriage but conceals more than she reveals. Through his characters, Megged also touches lightly on contemporary issues, such as pseudo-religious cults or guilt-ridden Germans who do volunteer work in Israel and are far more Zionist than the Israelis. Like many of Megged's novels, *The Honeymoons* is a satire of Israeli society, with Lunz both its target and its mouthpiece. As a scholar of Hebrew and other ancient languages, history is in his blood, and from that standpoint he laments "our [present] existential situation as Jews and as Israelis." Later, his condemnation intensifies—he denounces the cultural rot, the near-sightedness and lack of historical awareness that surround him. "I see the ground beneath our feet being destroyed and the roots that raised us torn out," he declares. Yet Lunz—Megged's protest against post-Zionism—is also full of satirical descriptions and plays with language in heartwarming ways.

Anat Feinberg

End the Occupation

Eli Amir, *Yasmin*
Tel Aviv, Am Oved, 2005. 411 pp.

In this country we talk a great deal about the "blood covenant" between Israel and the Druze. Eli Amir gives the term an entirely new interpretation. For him, this covenant is between an Israeli man and a Palestinian woman who make love while the woman is menstruating. In *Yasmin*, the bloodstained occupation of the Territories mingles with the bloodstained conquest of the Palestinian woman, they become one flesh and produce a moving love story. Nuri is what is known as an "enlightened occupier" in more ways than one. He is both the minister's advisor on Arab affairs in charge of the East Jerusalem office, and he is a conqueror by virtue of his love of Yasmin, a beautiful, intellectual Palestinian widow with a doctorate from the Sorbonne.

Hebrew literature is sadly lacking in novels dealing with binational love affairs. There are far more that deal with hatred. Stories of this kind, ending in heartbreak, occasionally appear in our newspapers, but they are usually about a love affair between an Israeli woman and an Arab man. *Yasmin* deals with an even greater taboo: an affair between an Israeli man and a Palestinian woman. Today, something like that could easily end in a death sentence for the woman, but even thirty-eight years ago Yasmin was accused of collaborating with the Zionists. The novel takes place in the euphoric period following the Six-Day War and Amir gives us a masterly portrait of the Israeli-

Palestinian conflict: on the one hand the changes in Israel, a country that went to bed under siege and woke up as an empire; on the other, Palestinian society in the wake of the occupation. Its conclusion is crystal clear and touches an exposed nerve in Israeli society: in its needless degradation of the Palestinian people, Israel has significantly contributed to increasing the hatred towards it.

Nuri speaks Arabic and understands the Palestinians' feelings. In his official capacity, he tries to be humane towards them (particularly to women), but comes up against a brick wall on the part of his superiors. As a result, the lovers find themselves in a situation where Yasmin can hope for nothing from her conservative society, and Nuri has no hope in his, even though it seems more progressive. Eli Amir himself is the son of Iraqi refugees from Baghdad who lived in an Israeli transit camp. In his eyes, he and his family—Jewish immigrants from Arab countries—share a similar fate to the Palestinians. This socio-political novel thus deals with two tragedies: that of the Palestinians under degrading Zionist occupation, and that of the Sephardim under humiliating Ashkenazi "occupation." And the message is: "End the Occupation."

At first Yasmin shies away from Nuri, but when she gets to know him she is enchanted that he knows the words of Umm Kulthoum's songs and the speeches of Nasser, whom she admires. The book begins in hatred, continues with a love that is "larger than life" and ends with the conclusion that a love of this sort is impossible in this country. After a night of lovemaking in the kibbutz where he grew up, Nuri drives Yasmin to her home. On the way they are stopped at a checkpoint where Yasmin has to go through a degrading body search. The checkpoint is also symbolic: it is a barrier against their love and the possibility that Yasmin, who has come back to Israel on a visit, will remain here.

Amir's mastery of contemporary Arabic gives him valuable access to its culture and poetry, and enables him to penetrate the deepest thoughts of his Palestinian protagonists. He is one of our best writers: in his work, the personal and the national are woven together, and he knows how to walk the tightrope between "I" and "we," drawing them together. This is particularly well done at the end of the novel, where the two merge and become indistinguishable. Ultimately, however, "I" prevails and gives us a heartbreaking ending.

Yaron Avitov

Surrealistic Mind Control

Miron C. Izakson, *The Flat on King Solomon Street*
Tel Aviv, Hakibbutz Hameuchad, 2004, 255 pp.

In his newest work, *The Flat on King Solomon Street*, poet and novelist Miron Izakson takes the reader into a strange Kafkaesque world, where the protagonists carry on mysterious, not entirely explained tasks. There is a constant consciousness of how the different parts of the body react to each situation—each part is anatomized and becomes an entity in itself.

The plot revolves around Uzi and Hana, an aging sister and brother who live together and even share the same double bed, since Hana's husband disappeared a while ago and Uzi's wife Tamari recently died. Hana, the older sister, organizes this living arrangement, much pleased to be living with her beloved younger brother and caring for him. She feels they have returned to the natural milieu of childhood, brother and sister having emerged from the same womb.

This cozy, well-ordered arrangement is threatened by the return of Amos, Uzi's son who is a member of a mysterious but powerful group in Europe that is called upon for its "professional" advice in life-death situations. Amos rules on issues of euthanasia, pulling the plug on someone in a coma, and whether a couple should conceive a child that might have a genetic disease. He is known for his cool logic, and the mastery of his mind over human circumstances.

Uzi who has waited anxiously for Amos to return to Israel,

pouts over the fact that he doesn't give him the attention that he gives people the world over. Izakson has created in Uzi a wonderful portrait of old age—cantankerous, feeling abandoned, hungry for sex and sweet things—as well as of his return to childhood.

But Uzi is attacked by a strange malady when Amos arrives and they go walking on the beach. He is cared for by Doctor Halamish, a renowned doctor who directs a laboratory for biological warfare and national security. Halamish has befriended Uzi and his sister, hoping to learn about Amos's methods of determining life and death. He seeks the intellectual control Uzi exhibits, the functioning of the mind without any compromise to the senses—all this to be used for the good of the state. But in order to win Amos over, he influences his assistant Mia to seduce him. The irony of the situation is that she teaches Amos to let go of his mental control and consciousness, and simply enjoy the pleasures of the body. They fall in love with each other, and at one point, take over Uzi and Hana's apartment.

Much of the subplot of the novel grapples with control over one's own mind and body, and control over others. There is Hana's control over her younger brother, Uzi's control over people's lives in fatal decisions, and Halamish's control of people for the good of the state. Protagonists are constantly disappearing and reappearing, part of the magical aura of the novel, but also a way of avoiding the controlling presence of others. Uzi's mother used to disappear every once in a while, until she disappeared altogether through her suicide. Uzi disappears from Israel for long periods of time, and Hana declares that she's going away in reaction to Amos and Mia taking over her home with their affair. But it is Uzi who steals the show from Hana by deciding to create a virtual funeral. He prepares for his funeral, so that he will have complete control over it and be able to observe it, rather than allow Amos to decide the parameters of his life and death as he's done for people all over the world. It is not clear, even to Uzi himself, whether he will go through with his funeral to the end. Covered with a prayer shawl, he is finally buried, but the book closes without the reader knowing whether he is buried dead or alive.

Izakson has created a surrealistic narrative that skews real-life situations, yet sheds light on life itself. His dreamlike sequences are compelling in that they develop a logic of their own, and confront the reader with profound philosophical and psychological issues.

Rochelle Furstenberg

Wise Questions

Nathan Shaham, *A Bell in Ch'ongiu*
Tel Aviv, Yedioth Ahronoth, 2005. 303 pp.

A Bell in Ch'ongiu is the story of an airplane hijacking turned hostage saga, lasting over 100 days on a remote island somewhere in South America. The identity of the hijackers is unclear at first; later on in the novel their connection to Palestinian terrorist organizations is gradually revealed. The hostages are First Class passengers on a flight from Athens to New York and it slowly becomes clear that the reason for their kidnapping is that they are all Jews. Only one of them is an observant Jew, a rabbi whose decisions remain with the reader for a long while.

The abduction occurs in 1969, and the story is that of one sur-vivor: a New York journalist and Pulitzer prize winner by the name of Joseph Schneider. Only in 1995 does he reconstruct his memories in writing. Why did he wait so long after his release from captivity? What kind of imprint has the experience left on him, and how has he changed since? In order to find out we must plunge into the heart of the book and Shaham's elaborate creation, for the plot is only the scaffolding on which he builds major questions, the kind that other authors avoid.

Shaham's insightful premise is that we have all seen and heard stories like these in such detail that we can dream them, reconstruct them and even turn off our TVs in the middle of yet another report. So what remains? Only what occurs where the public mind cannot reach, the remote island where nine hostages and a changing number of kidnappers spend day after day—first pitiably unaware of their jailers' objective and their own chances of survival, then as they slowly get to know one another and overcome distrust, and finally through an action plan that destroys the reader's hope for a peaceful conclusion.

Throughout all this, the novel leads its characters to reassess the clichés associated with a situation like this: at what point does humanity disintegrate? Is cohesiveness among hostages really possible, or does the tension between the "I" and the collective make it largely impossible? How does a complex relationship between kidnapper and hostage "really" develop, and is the Stockholm Syndrome an essential component of a work that deals with these questions?

The novel's strength lies in Shaham's wise and logical choice of artistic devices, which he controls extremely well. Small hints of future events; aphoristic, ironic writing well-suited to Shaham's protagonist; pushing emotional dramas to the periphery—all these enable the protagonist and his creator to make room for the theoretical questions at hand without preaching.

Is an experience like this ever over? In his epilogue, Shaham deals with this cliché with extraordinary wisdom and sensitivity. Abductor and abducted meet again many years later: both are condemned to carry this story with them, adding yet another layer to the reality they have changed through their decisions.

Ariana Melamed

Bliss in the Margins

Eitan Nahmias-Glass, *Lonely People Operas*
Tel Aviv, Achuzat Bayit, 2004. 207 pp.

Eitan Nahmias-Glass burst onto the Israeli literary scene in 1995 with his critically acclaimed poetry collection, *I am Simon Nahmias*. Adopting Simon Nahmias as his main speaker, Nahmias-Glass revealed an original, bold voice that challenged familiar ethnic stereotypes in Israeli society and portrayed life at its periphery.

In his first collection of short stories, Nahmias-Glass provides the narrative for the worlds his poetry touched upon. Although all the stories focus on families, the heroes are lonely people, many of them Holocaust survivors from Austria, Hungary and the Balkans. From the ghost of a seven year-old boy who died in the camps and now watches his father struggle with mundane life in Israel, to a sister who accidentally meets her long lost brother now a small time crook, the stories in this collection bring us a subtle, dark sarcasm and bitter-sweet plots. Most portray the ironies of fate: how something that happens returns to haunt the characters in the most unexpected places.

Thus, in "Bedtime Story," the narrator's mother recounts the story of her Albanian family during the Holocaust and how the woman who made their lives miserable in the camps returns as one of the sons' bride. Some characters find their redemption in their new land and life. The father in "Jacob's Dream," for example, discovers his dead son's picture only after he manages to connect with the living in the form of his cleaning lady. Others are ironically punished for their survivor mentality like the protagonist of "Lonely People's Operas" who, after longing for Europe and torturing those around him in Israel, sells all his property to move to Austria only to die penniless in Israel, an anti-hero.

Interestingly, although the different narrators and characters populating these stories live in Israel, they carry within them the voices, sights and smells of the (mostly) Sephardi diaspora. While they accept their new Israeli identity, they do not renounce their Jewish pasts as many immigrants to the newly established state did. Even native Israelis, like the brother and sister in "The Law of Great Returns,"—the longest story in the book—struggle with alienation. In their case, the incestuous relationship they are drawn into proves to be a desperate attempt at "family" happiness.

Throughout the book, Nahmias-Glass manages to portray these lives in the margins with great sensitivity and in a rich, poetic Hebrew that incorporates both the classics (like Agnon) and an ethno-linguistic collage reminiscent of the Sephardi-Israeli family novels of the 1990s. Perhaps the title of this collection—literally *Operas in a Heat Wave*—best reflects the opposing worlds it depicts, integrating distant pasts with the painful present while offering a glimpse of hope in the short moments of bliss they capture.

Hadar Makov-Hasson

Fictionalized History, Universal Humanity

Alon Hilu, *Death of a Monk*
Tel Aviv, Xargol, 2004. 250 pp.

Death of a Monk is a fictionalized account of a central event in 19th century Jewish history—the 1840 Damascus Affair—a blood libel in which the Jews of the city were accused of capturing and murdering an Italian monk and his Muslim servant, using their blood to make *matza,* the ritual Passover bread. The affair is recounted by one of the actual protagonists; his story, partly based on historical documentation, is the fruit of the author's imagination.

The novel's epigraph quotes Jewish socialist thinker Moshe Hess, who wrote in 1862: "Then came the event, reminding me that I am son to an unfortunate People, wrongfully accused; an outcast and abandoned People, dispersed and divided, but one that has not been destroyed." These lines clearly indicate the author's preoccupation with the Damascus Affair and its effect on the Zionist movement. However, the artistic choices Hilu makes in his novelistic adaptation illustrate his interest in one individual's perspective—that of Aslan Farhi, a young man grappling with his sexual identity, and struggling to find his place within his strict family and traditional community.

Aslan, the son of a wealthy merchant, has been forced to marry the daughter of the Chief Rabbi of Damascus and finds himself trapped in a loveless, miserable marriage. Submitting to a forbidden homosexual impulse, he becomes romantically involved with Mahmoud Altali, a Christian Arab in charge of investigating the monk's mysterious disappearance. He is also infatuated with Umm-Jihan, a beautiful singer whose bewitching voice and glamour mesmerize him. It is, however, Aslan's late-night rendez-vous with the monk Tomasso that propels the action of the novel, entangling him in a tragic web of deceit that leads to entrapment. A traitor to his people (we are later told that his Hebrew name is Yehuda, or Judas), Aslan fails to confess his pivotal role in the affair, which leads to the incarceration and torture of his immediate family as well as many other Jews, several of whom die in captivity.

As the gripping plot unravels, Hilu also gives us a masterful depiction of the colors, scents and scenes of 19th century Damascus— its vibrant markets, its winding alleys, its *hamam* and café offering forbidden pleasures, and its diverse population of Muslims, Christians and Jews. In this first novel, Hilu's rich and vivid prose, reminiscent of older literary Hebrew, serves his subject matter perfectly. Based on research and his Syrian parents' memories, Hilu's seamless amalgamation of history, religion and nationhood offers a profound exploration of human nature. His complex portrayal of Aslan mirrors our own passions and weaknesses: our need for love and a sense of belonging; our inclination towards the sinful and forbidden; our capacity for betrayal, and our ultimate need for acceptance and forgiveness.

Sharonne Cohen

No Ship of Fools

Michal Zamir, *A Ship of Girls*
Tel Aviv, Xargol, 2005. 191 pp.

It is no coincidence that Michal Zamir's new book drummed up interest as soon as it was released: this critical, somewhat subversive book attacks one of the pillars of the Israeli establishment—the army, which is undoubtedly one of the primary framers of Israeli identity.

Zamir tells the first-person story of an enlisted female soldier: "I haven't finished my two years [of army service], I'm not even 20 yet, and I've already had five abortions." It would seem she's done better than many since she serves—by virtue of family connections—in a military college where high ranking field officers come to get an academic degree. But her hopes of an interesting two years are quickly dashed, because the elite institution turns out to be a microcosm of sickness within the military and of the twisted morals of Israeli society at large. The "purity of arms" and "sanctity of the body," which are ingrained in soldiers from their first day of basic training, are exposed as a hollow slogan.

Zamir sketches a wide array of junior soldiers, officers and commanders who, beneath their façade of serious behavior and quiet authority, crave power and sex and are revealed as base and morally empty men. Brigadier General David Kochavi, a prime example of the type, accuses the protagonist—a former lover—as well as all the other female soldiers, "of screwing up our families, our kids and all enjoyment of our normal lives…given to us by the army. Or maybe it's the opposite. Maybe all of you are our consolation prize." Sex in Zamir's book is never dependent on love: this is a tale of sweat, urine, sperm, blood and vomit—all serving to accentuate a physical degeneration which mirrors moral decay.

Israeli women also come under attack in this book. The female soldier is drawn as a passive, submissive figure who "puts out" and serves the Israeli male. They are all either resigned to their fate, hungry for love, or hoping, at least once in their life, to be desired. Even motherhood is depicted as warped and doomed to failure: the narrator terminates her pregnancies; Alma, a soldier who decides to have a child "that has been fathered by the army," finds herself discharged from service; Michaela, who is supposed to attend officers' training course, commits suicide. And it is no coincidence that the narrator decides to neuter her dog Rachel, who seems to have got her name in a nod to irony—after the Biblical mother who paid with her life for her desire to have children.

The language of the book is fitting for a story that attacks the revered and beautiful, and maps out the painful and chilling side of Israeli society.

Anat Feinberg

Restoration through Story-Telling

Haim Sabato, *Like the Eyelids of the Morning*
Tel Aviv, Yedioth Ahronoth, 2005, 167pp.

Haim Sabato brings a unique spiritual voice to contemporary Hebrew literature. He does not talk about religion; instead, he gets into the mind and heart of the pious person. Like Agnon, Sabato draws figures from the Bible and his language resonates with religious sources; but unlike his predecessor whose work reflects the tension between tradition and modernism, Sabato is in harmony with the traditional world.

In *Like the Eyelids of the Morning*, his third novel, Sabato draws a portrait of Ezra Simantov, an old-time Sephardi Jerusalemite who is filled with wonder at God's world and the beauties of Torah and liturgy. He lives his Jerusalem life in the Mahane Yehuda market area, attends sunrise prayers and works in a laundry, ironing clothes and prayer shawls. He delights in his rabbi's sermons and the reciting of *piyuttim* the religious poems that elevate the spirit.

At first, Ezra Simantov may seem simpleminded, even Pollyannish, and Sabato's book overly sweet. But as the plot unfolds it becomes clear that the novel is many-layered, for Simantov's life is overshadowed by a terrible memory. When he was child he used to play ball with three friends, Moshe David, Yehuda Tawil and Rahamim. On one occasion, the ball flew over the wall into the forbidden territory of a monastery or hospital, and Moshe and Yehuda goaded Rahamim and Ezra to go and retrieve it. The two boys jumped over the wall and landed in what was probably a garbage dump, causing an explosion in which Rahamim lost his sight. After this, Ezra's life was never the same again. The other boys blamed him, and in the confusion of the moment, unable to remember exactly how the accident had happened, he accepted the blame.

Years later, Ezra Simantov still sees all the tragedies in his life as penance for that event, and for this reason he constantly tries to achieve *tikkun*, to restore the world to wholeness through his deeds. Weekly, he goes to clean Rahamim's room and hear the blind recluse play the violin. In a less direct way, he even sees ironing a suit that has seen better days as a means of *tikkun*. He is ridiculed for his simplicity by his learned friends, Moshe David and Yehuda Tawil. But these more accomplished acquaintances also need Ezra and his stories for their inspiration. Ultimately, Sabato presents story-telling itself as an act of *tikkun* that changes reality each time a tale is told. The Jerusalem that the author knows is sadly changing, but he too learns to accept it through the act of story-telling.

Rochelle Furstenberg

A Clerk of Small Human Sins

Shimon Adaf, *One Mile and Two Days before Sunset*
Jerusalem, Keter, 2004. 326 pp.

Shimon Adaf's very readable novel, *One Mile and Two Days before
Sunset*, situates itself simultaneously in the dusty streets of central
Tel Aviv and in the dusty projects of the southern towns Sderot and
Ashkelon. Disguised as a detective novel, the narrative depicts the
local rock scene, fragments of the academic world, and a generation
of young Israelis in search of identity and meaning.

To be sure, there is also a corpse, a couple of them actually.
One belongs to Dr. Yehuda Menuchin, an arrogant philosophy professor at Tel Aviv University. The other is that of Dalia Shushan, a
successful and talented rock singer and song writer. He committed
suicide, she was murdered, but as the protagonist detective, Elish
Ben Zaken, is quick to learn, things are much more complicated
than they seem.

The novel's greatest achievement is the intriguing character of
Ben Zaken. A brilliant intellectual in his thirties, he is incapable of
love and is haunted by a family tragedy from his past. After spending a few unsatisfying years in the university and publishing a book
on the rise and fall of Israeli rock music, Ben Zaken does his best to
withdraw from life. He becomes a partner in a private investigation
office, and presents himself as a "clerk of small human sins."

In a playful postmodernist manner, the novel juggles with
concepts of authenticity, creativity and the very act of writing. For
example, both the title and the epigraph are taken from popular songs
written by the fictive character, Dalia Shushan. In the course of the
investigation, Ben Zaken travels back and forth from Tel Aviv to
Sderot and Ashkelon, and is forced to face some of his own childhood
demons. The novel goes beyond this physical geography to suggest
that notions of center and periphery are in fact internal and stem

from each person's unique individuality. In the process, it creates a sharp and sensitive depiction of the margins of Israeli society.

Shiri Goren

Angst and Rivalry

Israel Segal, *My Brother's Keeper*
Jerusalem, Keter, 2004. 249 pp.

Two brothers: ancient mythology, ancient Egyptian literature, the Bible and various legends all include tales of two brothers, their love and hatred, the way their paths cross and diverge. In his third novel, Israel Segal enters this fertile field and reverts once again to his inner world and his relationship with his brother.

This is unquestionably a powerful, gripping book. It is about the drama of an ultra-Orthodox family in which the older brother becomes a shining example to his community while the younger brother, a "black sheep," leaves it. The dichotomy is not simple. The older brother withdraws from worldly pleasures to become the ultra-Orthodox ideal, while the latter withdraws from his origins into the secular world with all its disorders and temptations. And there is deep conflict between them. Does it come only from the fact that the two brothers have adopted opposing life-styles, or are there other reasons, which make their respective choices a result rather than a cause?

When a novel is built on a psychological approach, the question of cause is central, and there is no dearth of material. The parents are deeply estranged and each one carries hurt. The birth of the younger son was supposed to bring renewal—even atonement—to the mother and her elder son, to be a mystical event. But a blessing of this sort may also hide a curse: siblings can be a source of envy and hostility, and the curse is handed down to the children by their parents.

When parents eat sour grapes, the teeth of the sons are set on edge and there is no remedy. From a remote father will grow a reclusive son and from an unstable mother, a son who is torn between two worlds. Here, the brothers are separated by the distance which kept their parents apart, and more.

Israel Segal has written a beautiful and horrifying book. He makes maximum narrative use of the dramatic materials at his disposal and weaves them into an impressive fabric. His Hebrew has a dramatic force all its own, as befits a writer who draws deeply on Jewish sources and is attuned to the power of Hebrew syntax. With touching sincerity, Segal creates a balance between the "big questions" relating to faith, Providence and the world order, and everyday life with its mundane desires. A considerable part of the book's beauty lies in the extreme polarities it portrays, for children of the same parents can never be totally detached from one another.

Why did Cain murder Abel? The debate continues to this day. Abel died and Cain was condemned to live with the mark that singled him out as a murderer. He was also condemned to carry the reason for the murder deep in his heart for ever, while Abel was condemned to be the silent *tzaddik*, the righteous one. Segal draws inspiration from this and other aspects of Jewish lore and strives to attain a mythical tone and dimension on the basis of a story about one family and two sectors of Israeli society. Indeed, for the heroes, these events are not mythic but all too real, even many years later.

Ioram Melcer

The Mysterious Ivanov

David Tarbay, *Stalker*
Tel Aviv, Am Oved, 2004. 198 pp.

A boy lives meagerly among a small, persecuted group of people. The historical time is vague and the place is known only as the "Zone," but it resembles an internment camp or a deserted army base. In this community, relationships are based purely on function and usefulness—an irritable old lady gives cooking and sewing classes; a teenage girl assists her; an old professor who is building a strange machine teaches the boy science and Roman history in exchange for bullets; and another man, Ivanov, carries out any task that demands physical strength or daring.

The particulars of this world are surreal but its mood is familiar. Many of the worst aspects of our world can be found there: oppression, uncertainty, natural disaster, apathy, sickness and aging. Even generosity is random, its motivation unclear, as with the food packages left in the shadow of the guard towers. The community don't know who leaves them there; why, at times, people are shot when they approach them, or why their content is old and rotten. But even here we find a touch of goodness, and nearly all of it comes from the active imagination of the boy. When the girl, Layla, goes out with him to play a few games, his imagination turns them into enchanted journeys; when a stray dog joins the group, he calls it Swan after the character in *Lohengrin* that Ivanov told him. And in this harsh reality, the boy's imagination even creates hope—he conjures up a huge, powerful figure who will free them all. His name is Stalker.

A fantastic episode involving the professor's machine transports the boy and his companions to a new surrounding, but it is similar to the Zone. From there the story continues to modern-day London, where Ivanov is now a famous conductor. His new surroundings look modern and well-organized, but beneath the surface it, too, functions in the same way as the Zone.

Is the Ivanov at the end of the book the boy from the beginning? Is the boy that Ivanov meets at the end the one that appeared in middle? Does Ivanov's return to the Zone represent the duality most people feel towards their youth? Does art—in this case music—replace the hopes of youth? David Tarbay holds the answers. *Stalker* is an allegory open to the reader's interpretation, and that may be a limitation. Readers who don't have the mental or emotional stamina may not understand Tarbay's complex narrative. But that challenge is the novel's greatest strength, for the reader is invited to carry his Ivanov to his own private Zone, to his Swan which strangers may see only as a dog. Mainly, the reader is drawn into a highly aesthetic reading experience where prose mingles with the raw materials of life…

At its best, literature reflects the reader's world from an unsuspected angle. *Stalker* does this in an impressive and enjoyable way.

Amnon Jackont

Post-Zionist Perspective with Humor

Asher Kravitz, *I, Mustafa Rabinovitch*
Tel Aviv, Sifriat Poalim, 2004. 164 pp.

Who is the enemy, the hated "other" that Israelis fight but cannot beat? This is the question that underlies Asher Kravitz's third novel. Kravitz, a physicist and native of Jerusalem, was born in 1969 and served in the IDF during the 1ˢᵗ Intifada (1987–1993). He tells the first-person story of Yair Rabinovitch, a member of an elite undercover unit whose brief is to find, arrest and kill wanted terrorists. On the job, Yair is known as Mustafa, but this borrowed identity takes on additional meaning during the novel: "The hands are the hands of Mustafa and the voice is the voice of Rabinovitch," reflects the biblical Isaac's words when he was tricked into blessing his disguised younger son, Jacob. During a brief respite from the army, when Yair is in hospital with a minor injury, he comes to realize that his knowledge of Palestinians is superficial. Even if he does know how "Palestinians brush their teeth," he observes them "like a swarm of ants." Later on, Yair goes back to Nablus without his disguise because he wants to see reality from the other side, through the eyes of the locals. And there, he discovers the misery, helplessness and hopelessness of the "enemy."

But the strength of this novel does not only come from its theme. After all, the stories of S.Yizhar deal with the moral dilemma of an Israeli torn between country and conscience, and we can find empathy towards Palestinian society in the work of David Grossman and Yitzhak Laor. No, the power of this novel lies in the perspective of the narrator, Yair, who avoids pathos, uses self-reflective irony, and tries—usually successfully—to avoid the pitfalls of stereotype. Yair's personal life adds an interesting twist to the question of the "other." His favorite author is not Israeli, but a Yiddish-speaking diaspora Jew, Isaac Bashevis Singer. And his admiration for Singer's novels, in turn, brings him close to Hadas, who studies Chinese and is in charge of the monkey rehabilitation farm on her kibbutz. She does not reject him like Abigail, the hospital nurse, did. But he fails anyway, for she is only playing with him, like with all her lovers. Written in a fluid style, with a sense of humor verging on the absurd, Kravitz ultimately portrays the Israeli as a loser, drifting in uncertainty and post-Zionist atheism.

Anat Feinberg

Straight from the Heart

Avram Kantor, *Leading Voice*
Tel Aviv, Hakibbutz Hameuchad, 2004. 176 pp.

The unnamed narrator of this novel is a thoughtful 12 year-old boy facing the typical complexities and angst of adolescence: discovering the opposite sex, recognizing the tell-tale signs of sexual development, having to assert selfhood and identity within a harsh, sometimes ruthless social order. What makes his story compelling is an added challenge: he is unable to express himself as most people do—with his voice.

Although he is capable of making sounds with his teeth, tongue and lips, the narrator cannot use his vocal chords, a fact that has troubled his parents throughout his life. They have taken their son to countless experts, all providing diagnoses that don't correspond to the parents' intuitive sense that their son is not autistic or socially impaired. They know he is able to communicate—and he does. He develops the ability to communicate through gestures, facial expressions, and other non-verbal signs. He has an especially meaningful rapport with his father, who seems to understand his thoughts and feelings even by looking into his eyes.

The narrator's older sister, while learning the alphabet and practicing her reading, unknowingly teaches him how to read at a very young age. Infinitely curious, and also aware of the importance of verbal communication in social interaction, he later uses his brother's computer to secretly learn how to write, mastering the computer's software that also enables him to browse the Internet and snoop into his brother's surfing activities. He supplements the knowledge he finds on the Web through his mother's books, learning not only about his condition (what it is, and—more importantly—what it is not), but also about human sexuality and various other subjects. But he chooses to keep his reading and writing skills a secret—from his family, his teachers, and from the "experts" evaluating him.

When Kobi, the narrator's almost 18 year-old brother, who is about to be drafted into the army, begins showing interest in Jewish laws and practices, the narrator finds clues that lead him to the conclusion that his brother has made contact with an ultra-Orthodox community, which is about to tear him away from his secular family. Unbeknownst to his parents and sister, he sets out on a mission to return his brother home, "saving" him from the religious brainwashing he believes his brother is undergoing.

Written with sensitivity and compassion, this novel provides a glimpse into a world most of us know little about, shedding light on human interaction, and also provoking thoughts about our understanding of the possibilities of communication. It is also a metatextual reminder of the joy of reading, of absorbing new knowledge, and of discovering new frontiers.

Sharonne Cohen

Daycare for the Chronically Forgetful

Gai Ad, *7 Harimon Street*,
Tel Aviv, Zmora Bitan, 2004. 174 pp.

The blooming of "outsider" literature is one of the most fascinating trends of recent decades. Books by or about immigrants and children of immigrants from Asia (Salman Rushdie, Hanif Kureishi, Amy Tan, and so on) have starred on bestseller lists and won literary prizes in the West. The "outsider" child with unusual tendencies has also become a popular hero in fiction—see the sensational success of Harry Potter, or Mark Huddon's *The Curious Incident of the Dog in the Night*, narrated by an autistic adolescent who captured readers' hearts.

Missing from the "outsiders" brought into the spotlight are the elderly—especially those who suffer from diseases and mental disorders. Western culture often views advanced age as a condition more dreadful than any malignancy. But as it turns out, a heartwarming, even optimistic book can be written about both the elderly and disease. To make that happen you need to love people, to be a skillful writer and to have the intuitive intelligence of Gai Ad, the author of the slim and charming novel, *7 Harimon Street*.

The heroes of this novel are incurable mental and Alzheimer patients in the evening of their lives. It is easy to fall in love with them. They have fascinating life stories, and they know how to love, feel, and touch more than "standard-issue" young people who have learned to suppress their emotions. In *My Michael*, Amos Oz warns that if you cultivate feeling and become addicted to it, it may become a "malignant tumor." But Gai Ad's characters teach us that untamed feelings are the power of life. Healthy young people, like the narrator who has just returned from a long stint in the USA with a "dense emptiness," can learn from this. She and her friends start a daycare center for the elderly, and as her "dense emptiness" comes into contact with their feelings, they become closer. She draws strength from them and they become a substitute family for her.

One of the fascinating things about this book is that it gives us the opportunity to enter the patients' inner world as they try to impose order and sequence on the chaos in their minds. Imposing order is the beginning of all thought, invention and art. Sadly, unlike inventors and artists, the sick are unable to do this. And yet there is a heartwarming creativity in their chaos, like the moving slip a patient makes when he asks for butter on his "pity-bread" for breakfast.

It is to be hoped that Gai Ad's wonderful book will do for the elderly and infirm what Mark Huddon's *Curious Incident of the Dog* did for the autistic. Hopefully it will save them from the exile to which they are condemned in our society.

Miri Paz

The fonts used in this book are from the Garamond family